Going Monstering

Going Monstering

By

Edward Lee

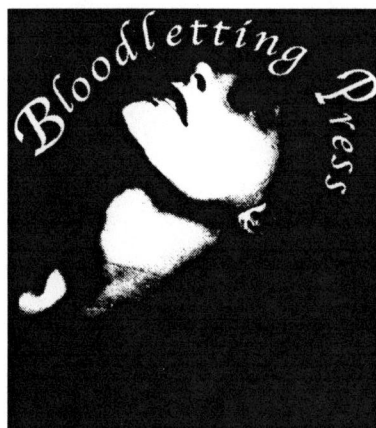

2011

YOU girls'll want coffee, I take it?" Kezzy asked. She came around the kitchen table with that big bright phony smile of hers, holding the pot. It's a smile I'd get to know well.

"Oh, yes, thank you, Miss Kezzy!" the skinny chick said. Her name was Mercy Dexter and she was so skinny I don't know how she bought clothes. I wished I could be skinny too but, shit, not *that* skinny. We found out real quick she was one of those Bible-thumping holy rollers — for fuck's sake. Oh, and she wore a big cross like the one Ozzy Osborne wears. All three of us were nerds, but Mercy was a *Super Nerd*. Ink-black hair, bangs, gawky. The kind of girl a novelist would call "mousy" or "librarianish" 'cos he didn't feel like thinking of something better.

"Sure, I'd love some, Miss Kezzy," the second "initiate" said. Her name was Hannah Bowen and I knew her from orientation a couple months ago. She was all right, I guess, a little snooty 'cos her folks were rich but, shit, *all* of our folks were rich. How else could we get into a private girls' college? One thing I liked about Hannah was her glasses looked worse than mine. You know, Coke bottles. But what I liked most was that she weighed more than me. I weighed 190 at five-foot four, and she was over 200, but the kick in the ass was she didn't *look* as fat 'cos she was almost six feet tall. Guys called her Sasquatch behind her back. "I've always been a coffee drinker!" she said, like it was a big deal.

Next, Kezzy's phony smile swerved to me, like a flashlight beam in my face. "And you, Ann?"

"Ann" would be me, Ann White. I'm fat, uninteresting, and morose. No brag, just fact. I'm a pot-head, I drink too much, and at 19 years of age I have less motivation than an old person on their death bed. My belly turns into six rolls of fat — serious, I counted 'em — whenever I sit down, and one time I was walking down the street and some dude I never seen before says, "Hey, baby, I didn't know they *made* blue jeans for elephants!" Just like that, out of the blue. Another time I was actually on a "date," and when we were making out, the guy opens my blouse, but when he took a look at my tits, he started laughing. The fucker wouldn't stop. "Sorry, Ann, I can't help it!" he kept hee-hawing. "It's just that your tits... look ridiculous!" How do you like that shit, huh? I gave him a blowjob anyway 'cos he had pot, which I guess gives you an idea of just how fucked up I am. Oh, and my hair? Looks like somebody plugged me into a wall socket, and it's the color of... well, you ever see a white poodle that's got away for a couple weeks, so it's all dirty and mangy? *That's* what my hair looks like. Thanks a lot, God.

Anyway, as to the coffee offer, I said, "Yeah. Anything with caffeine."

She kind of froze, glaring at me. "What was that, Ann?"

Asshole, I thought. "Yeah, anything with caffeine, *Miss Kezzy.*"

"Better," she said. See, she has this superiority thing. Mere pledges must always show respect to senior "sisters." She poured three cups, her perfect teeth gleaming like that stupid commercial with the Australian chick or some shit. Kezzy Mason was the S.S.S. — the Senior Sorority Sister — so it was her ass we had to kiss if we wanted to get into Alpha House. She made me sick the first minute I saw her. You know, the phony smile, the Fuck You face, the *perfect* body, the *perfect* blond hair. The bitch looked like Pam Anderson but, like, when Pam Anderson was fuckin' 20.

"You girls will just *love* this coffee. It's Costa Rican!"

Big fuckin' deal.

"Oh, and Mercy, dear?" Kezzy raised her finger. "Since you haven't yet been fully initiated, it's understandable that you're not familiar with the Alpha House dress code, but I'm afraid you'll have to lose the cross."

Mercy's skinny face kind of twisted up like someone just told her that her whole family got killed in a car wreck. Her skinny hand reached up and touched the cross. "You can't make me get rid of my cross..."

"I have no desire to make you get *rid* of it," Kezzy came back. She had a way of talking that reminded me of scissors. Snip, snip, snip. "I'm simply informing you that your cross is considered a violation of our dress code."

"But, but, I'm a Christian! Christians wear crosses!"

"That may well be, but what you must understand is that Christians who wear crosses in Alpha House, just as any girl who wears *any* unauthorized jewelry, are not *admitted* into Alpha House." Kezzy stared, tapping a foot. "You *do* want to be in this sorority, don't you?"

"Well, well, yes, but, but, I should be able to wear my cross. It's the symbol of my Lord and Savior!"

"Fine. Then you can take yourself along *with* the symbol of your Lord and Savior out of this house right now and never come back."

Silence. What a bad scene right off the bat. But it got worse when Hannah's eyes narrowed and she said, "That seems fairly discriminatory, Miss Kezzy."

Kezzy's glare snapped to Hannah. "Does it, now? Discriminatory? It's a good thing for you we don't discriminate against

7

girls with 1.3 grade-point averages, hmm?"

Hannah's mouth fell open. "You didn't have to say that in *front* of everybody!" Her shitty grades were something she tried hard to keep from others. A pride thing. So she'd lie about them just like she lied about her weight, "boyfriends" she'd never really had, how she was the darling of her rich family when she was actually the clunker. You know the type.

"What about you, Ann?" Kezzy's gaze felt like an ice-cold draft. "Do you feel I'm being discriminatory, *you* meaning a girl with a 1.2 average?"

"No, Miss Kezzy," I sucked right up. "Mercy, take the cross off. Rules are rules. Jesus isn't gonna condemn you to hell for obeying the rules, is He?"

"Well, no," she peeped. "He does know that I'm His faithful servant."

"Good. So take it off. And Hannah, you need to get into a sorority as bad as I do, so why not...appeal to Miss Kezzy's good nature and say you're sorry for implying that she's discriminatory?"

Hannah — the pussy — wiped a tear out of her eye. "I'm sorry, Miss Kezzy."

We all looked at Mercy. She gulped and took off the cross.

Kezzy smiled. "Good!"

Time out, just so you get the gist. Girls always have their own reasons for wanting to get into a sorority, but nine times out of ten it's got something to do with family. You have to *prove* something to your family, you have to *prove* to them that you can fit in the way *they* did when they were in college; you have to give them something to yack about at dinner parties, you know, "Oh, my daughter so-and-so is in the best sorority!" It indicated *refinement* or some shit. The fact was, me, Hannah, and Mercy were three misfits who'd been turned down by every house on the row. Mercy wanted in because her parents told her they'd stop paying for college if she didn't "socialize" more, said her obsession with church was making her too introverted, and even though her grades were average, her dad didn't want to spend the bucks just to have his daughter wind up in a convent holding a $200,000 degree. With Hannah, it was her sisters. Three princesses, and she was the ugly ducking. They were *all* in sororities, and she was sick to death of her parents always asking her why she couldn't be like her sisters. My reason's more blunt. My folks are pigshit rich, but they "won't stand" to have an "under-achiever" for a daughter. "A little motivation's what you need," my dad said to me when I eked out my high school diploma after getting an academic waiver—which dad *paid* for—and then I got busted on graduation night for buying pot. (Oh, and I gotta add that blowjobs were more the reason I graduated, not studying.) The short version? Dad gave me the ultimatum: "Graduate from college or you're out of the will." Shit, that inheritance is *the only thing* I got going for me. He and mom both smoke and drink bigtime, so, shit, they'll both probably be in the ground by the time they're fifty. But if I don't pass college they're gonna leave everything to—can you believe it?—the fuckin' Salvation Army. So it was sink or swim time for me, and I'd been pretty much sinking my whole life. Now, you're probably wondering something like, *What's she talking about? Getting into a sorority can't guarantee a college diploma.*

I'll get to that part in a bit.

Anyway, the air cleared after the fuss about the cross, and Kezzy put her phony smiling fuck-you face right back on like nothing happened. Remember, she'd just poured the coffee, so now she asked, "I trust you girls would all like cream?"

"Lots of cream, yes, Miss Kezzy," Hannah said. "And sugar, please, thank you."

"Just a little cream for me, please, Miss Kezzy," said the sulking Mercy.

My turn. "I'd prefer mine black, Miss Kezzy."

She scowled. "So. *You're* the maverick now, Ann? Everyone *else* wants cream, but *you* don't? Are you too *good* to have cream like the rest of the girls? Hmm?"

Going Monstering

Oh, for fuck's sake! "I'm sorry, Miss Kezzy. I meant that I *do* want cream."

"Good." Snip. She glanced over her shoulder toward the door. "Zenas!"

NOW what? I thought. I dared to speak. "Um, Miss Kezzy? Who's Zenas, if I may ask?"

"Why, Zenas is the maid, Ann."

"Isn't, uh, isn't the name Zenas a *man's* name? An old name from Colonial days? Old Yankee, or whatever they call it?"

"Yes, it is."

Me, Hannah, and Mercy all looked at each other, but I was the one who kept talking. "You mean the Alpha House *maid...* is a *man?*"

"That's correct, Ann," but then she shot a glare toward Hannah. "You see, we don't *discriminate* here."

I guess I suspected that shit was seriously fucked up all along, you know, subconsciously. But there was no doubt when the kitchen door swung open, and in walked this brawny, strapping, ox-necked guy with biceps that looked like fuckin' mangoes. He had kind of greasy rednecky hair and serious five o'clock shadow. But, see, it's what he was *wearing...*

He was wearing a *maid's* outfit.

"Oh, my gosh!" Mercy squealed, and she was actually laughing. She thought it was a joke.

"Come on!" Hannah exclaimed. "What kind of gag is this?"

But, me? I think I'd already gotten the idea because I'd heard all the stories about "hazing." All I said was "Oh, fuck."

"Zenas," Kezzy introduced. "Meet our three new pledges. Mercy, Hannah, and Ann."

"Hey-yuh, girlies. En't a bad place ta live'n dew yew're larnin', eh?" the guy said in the heaviest New England redneck accent I ever heard. No lie, this rube was decked out in the real deal: black stockings, the short fringy petticoat thing, a serving apron, laced cuffs, even a fuckin' bodice and matching pumps. And I could tell right off the bat he was no swish. It had to be another one of Kezzy's gigs; you'll know what I mean later, about how she *loved* to demean people. But even before it happened I knew what was going on here, which tells you just how deep in the gutter my mind lives. "Miss Kezzy? May I ask the maid a question?"

"Of course, Ann."

I couldn't help eyeballing the guy's pecs bulging through the black bodice. "Zenas, why's a gorgeous meat-rack like you dressed up like a French maid? Ain't no way you're gay, ain't no way you're a transvestite. So..."

He shot his pecs, then—I guess it's called pronation—*pronated* his arms to show off the triceps. "Kezzy, she pays me some long coin, ee-yuh. Whud'jew think, fattie?"

You have no idea how much I appreciated the "fattie."

"Zenas is compensated one thousand dollars per week to serve as Alpha House's maid. He's also quite a serviceable housekeeper, cook, and driver."

Somehow I figured he was also a quite serviceable cock vendor, reserved exclusively for Kezzy.

"This is ridiculous!" Hannah said. "I can't believe he's dressed up like that!"

Mercy just kept giggling.

Kezzy gave her most smug smile yet. "Zenas. Pour the cream."

"Wuz hopin' yud ask. En't got one off since yestuh-dee, new suh," he gruffed and kind of hitched his hips when he slipped down the pantyhose and pulled out a cock that looked like something hanging in a deli. Then, right there in front of us, he began to beat off.

Mercy screamed like a train whistle, and Hannah, she brought her hands to her face like that Edvard Munch painting that got stolen. But me?

I just pursed my lips and nodded.

Zenas kept whipping his flaccid cock until it started to go. The fuckin' thing *had* to be ten inches, and it was about as thick

11

as a can of Red Bull. I'd seen some off-the-wall shit in my life, but this? Shit. For some reason, it wouldn't have been quite so bad if he hadn't been wearing the maid suit. And the sound of the guy jerking off was like someone slapping raw burger.

Hannah just sat there, open-eyed and open-mouthed, but Mercy squealed, "What, what is he *doing!*"

Kezzy looked to me. "Ann, you seem to be more cognizant than the others. Why don't you tell our naive friend here what he's doing?"

I rubbed my face. "He's gonna come in the coffee cups, Mercy. And we gotta drink it."

Mercy looked like someone just walked right up to her and kicked her in the cunt. "What? *Come?* What do you mean?"

"He's going to *ejaculate* in our coffee, bonehead. It's a sorority prank, you know. *Cream in your coffee?* Get it?"

"No!" she wailed. "You mean like, like...*sperm?*"

"Yeah, Mercy. Sperm. Dicksnot. Man-batter. So just...get ready."

They watched in shock as Zenas began to huff and twitch. It really was the most ludicrous thing I've ever seen: a grown man in a maid's outfit, jerking off in *coffee.* Eventually the guy's nuts bunched up, and then he—what's the word? He *inclined* his pelvis over the table edge, and said, "Cream on the way..." He fired two big spurts into Mercy's cup, grunted, "Two fuh yew, string bean," then two into the second cup, "Two fuh yew, Bigfoot," then...

The asshole rips *five* spurts off into *my* cup.

"Eeee-YUH. Extra cream fuh Jobbessa the Hut."

This guy's load was so thick it looked like Udon noodles coming out of his dick. My karma, I'll tell you. Oh, and I really appreciated that Jobbessa crack.

Hannah kept looking shell-shocked, and Mercy was *vibrating* in her seat. Meanwhile, Zenas slapped the rest out on the table, and it was like someone slapping a pork loin down. Then he shoved all his deflated junk back into his pantyhose. "Theer's yer cream, ladies," and then he laughed. There were little wisps of white film floating on top, but I knew what was sitting in the bottom...

Jesus Christ, Mercy was *crying* now. She pointed to the cups with a shaking finger. "We, we...we have to...*drink* it?"

"'Fraid so," I said. "Miss Kezzy didn't go to all this trouble just to have us look at it."

"Maybe, maybe," Hannah stuttered, "maybe we really don't have to. Like maybe, maybe, Miss Kezzy just wants to gross us out. And maybe, like, just before we're *about* to drink it, she'll say we don't have to."

At that remark, we all looked up to Kezzy. The expression on her face was like a fuckin' bust of Napoleon.

"I wouldn't count on that," I said.

"But why?" Mercy kept wailing. "Why do we have to drink it?"

"It's *hazing*, Mercy," I told her. "That's just the way it is, it's tradition. It you want to get into a sorority, you have to go through an initiation period. When our parents were in college, they'd have to do stuff like moon the dean, or toilet-paper the police station, pull a jock-trap raid, or walk around with a dunce hat for a week, candy-ass stuff like that. But in *this* day and age, it's different. You gotta eat a banana you wiped your ass with, run across the quad naked, fuck a guy on the dean's front yard, or, or — "

I pointed to the coffee cups.

Kezzy crossed her arms and tapped her foot. "I'm waiting, girls. Would you like to sit here all day, or would you like to see your room?"

I sighed. (I'd be sighing a lot over the next week.) "Come on. Let's just do it. We *have* to do it."

"I'm not drinking coffee with sperm in it!" Mercy wailed. "I've never even *seen* sperm before, much less *tasted* it!"

"Neither have I!" Hannah added.

"Oh, fuck you, Hannah!" I yelled. "You've sucked plenty of

dicks. You told me so!"

"I can't *believe* you just told them that!"

"Look," I tried to reason. "If we don't do it, we're out. It all ends right here the first day, then we go back to our loser lives and we'll be flunked out by the end of next semester. So let's just do it and get it *over* with."

"But I'm a Christian!" Mercy shrieked. "I can't drink coffee with *sperm* in it! It's a sin!"

"Bullshit, Mercy. Does it say that in the Bible? Does it specifically *say* you can't drink coffee with sperm in it?"

"Well, well, no, but—"

"Did somebody pull a stone tablet out of a bush that said Thou shalt not drink coffee with sperm in it?"

Her lower lip trembled. "Well. No..."

"Then shut up, stop whining, stop being a pain in the ass, and drink the goddamn coffee!" I yelled at her.

"You didn't have to use the Lord's name in vain!" she sobbed.

"Oh, for fuck's sake," I mumbled.

Kezzy's foot continued to tap. "So, girls? How many of you are weaklings and how many of you are Alpha House material? Make up your minds now. No one's forcing you to stay. Is Ann the only one who truly wants to be in this sorority? Hmm? Well, I'll give you to the count of three. One... Two..."

I picked up my cup.

"Oh my God, oh my God!" Hannah groaned.

"I don't think I *can*!" Mercy squealed next.

"Three."

I swallowed my coffee in one gulp, and could feel all that cum floating down with it. Then I slammed the cup on the table and looked at the others.

Mercy and Hannah's faces were shriveled up like prunes, but believe it or not, they chugged theirs down too. Mercy actually fell back in her chair and hit the floor, and Hannah started hacking.

"Congratulations, girls," Kezzy told us. "You've passed the first test." Her foot tapped. "Now let's see how many of you have the fortitude to pass the rest."

☠ ☠ ☠

ASIDE from having a dirty mouth, I've got a *big* mouth. I was never "pretty" so I grew up like a Tom Boy, I guess they call it, and for some reason trash-talk always stuck to me. I'm like some punk, pain-in-the-ass teenage boy from a trailer park clap-trapping around all the time on a skateboard and cussing, but I've got the body of a fat *girl*. Dad's money's the only thing that got me into a school like this.

The school's called Dunwich Women's College, and it's very much a private institution. Huge tuitions, no scholarships, no athletic programs, nothing like that. Rich girls who couldn't get into to Harvard or Yale went to Dunwich 'cos they didn't care about GPA's for the first semester. Lotta parents packed their daughters off here because they knew they couldn't get into much trouble. The nearest coed college was fifty miles away. Daddy knew he could send Princess to Dunwich and not worry about her getting knocked up. Nearest decent-sized town was Wilbraham, like, seventy miles west, and even *that's* about as dull as dull gets. Dunwich was in the sticks, in other words. There was, like, *nothing* to do off campus. The location kept the girls out of mischief, or I should say the girls in any sorority but Alpha House.

Because my high school grades were so low, when the first semester starts here next week, I'll be on academic probation. That means I get *one more semester* to get my grades up, or I'm out. And that's what I want to get to next — the deal with Alpha House's rep for helping girls get their grades up. But I'll tell you

Going Monstering

about the house first.

Alpha House looks like every other house on Greek Row. Old but well-tended, white-painted brick, big bow windows, plus second-story dormers sticking out of the roof. It's also got these stone pillars across the front porch. I guess *stately* is the word. Only weird thing is the letter A on the door looks more Arabic than Greek, and there's this word on a little brass plaque just underneath it that says *Azif* in cursive letters, almost as if they're saying it's Azif House, not Alpha House. But I'd seen the inside of just about every other sorority house during application week, *then* I saw the inside of Alpha House. All I can say is *holy* FUCK. It blows every other house away by a mile. It even looks better than the inside of my *parents'* house, and *that* hell-hole cost six million. I'm talking the best furniture, the best carpet, the best fixtures, the best everything. *Giant* crystal chandelier in the foyer. Statues and oil paintings all over the place; huge plasma TV's all over the place, too, even in the bathrooms, and the fuckin' bathrooms look like something you'd expect in Bill Gates' house. Shit, they've got *heated toilet seats*. When I asked Kezzy why this sorority house was so much fancier inside than the other houses, the snooty bitch said it's 'cos of contributions from Alpha House alumni. Well, all I can say to that is she's talking *serious* contributions. Oh, and the Alpha House car? It's a Rolls fuckin' Royce. No bullshit.

Anyway, here's the deal with the grades — the matriculation rate or whatever they call it. See, Alpha House has its own tutoring program. Any girl who gets admitted to the sorority, if she's got shitty grades, the tutors help her. Kezzy even showed us the stats: *Every single Alpha House sister*, since, like the 1800's when the school was founded, graduated with honors. No exceptions. They all got 4.0 averages.

No exceptions.

So with stats like that, I figured even a lazy, unmotivated loaf like me could get a college degree, and with a college degree?

Edward Lee

Dad would keep me in the will.

That's why getting into Alpha House meant so much to me. In fact, it meant more to me than anything else in the world. Any girl could get into the sorority if they passed all the tests during pledge week, but not any girl could *apply*. Here's where I lucked out—and it's pretty fucked up, too, and after the cum in the coffee thing, you're already getting the gist that there's a *whole lot* that's fucked up about Alpha House.

See, you have to be a virgin to get in. Kid you not—a *virgin*. It's the first question on the fuckin' application: ARE YOU A VIRGIN? It sounded like more pledge foolishness to me—like if a girl lied and said yes, how could they check? A fuckin' lie-detector, or hypnosis, or a GYN exam? But for me it didn't matter because, technically, I *was* a virgin. I've blown a lot of guys, sure, and I've taken it in the rear a bunch of times, too (shit, a *whole bunch* of times), but since there's never been a penis in my vagina, as far as I'm concerned, that makes me a virgin. So I didn't even have to lie on the app, as ridiculous as the whole thing was. If you're a fat girl in this day and age, you pretty much *have* to suck dick if you want guys to have anything to do with you, and you've got to take it up the ass, too. If some dude had *wanted* to put it in my pussy, I'm sure I would've gone for it. But no one ever did. And I know the reason. It's the "fat girl" thing. To most guys, if you're a fat girl, you're desperate, and guys *like* the desperation element. They also like the degradation element; it turns them on. "Yeah, I cornholed a fat girl last night, har-har-har," they'd tell their buddies like it was a badge of honor. Or, "Blew a load right down the fat bitch's throat, and the 'ho loved it." That sort of thing. It's really depressing that people can even be that way, that they can *disregard* you that much, just because you're fat and most everyone else is beautiful. But the most depressing part of all is me going along with it. Usually the guys had pot or beer so, sure, but mostly? It's because I was lonely.

Pathetic, huh?

17

Going Monstering

Anyway, there you have it. I was a virgin only by circumstance, and that turned out to be my good luck as far as Alpha House went. In fact, now that I think on it, it was the first time in my life I'd ever had an advantage over anybody; it's not like 19-year-old virgins grew on trees. Hannah was pretty much in the same boat; she'd never been fucked 'cos no guy'd ever wanted to fuck her. But she'd blown her share of dudes for the same reason as me, and taken it up the butt a few times, too — not that she'd ever admit it. And Mercy? Christ, all you had to do was *look* at her to know she was a virgin. I doubt she'd ever even kissed a guy. To her, any intimacy out of wedlock was a sin. I wouldn't be surprised if we were the only three virgins on the whole fuckin' campus. And it didn't matter if the whole virgin thing turned out to be a sham — all I cared about was having a chance to get into Alpha House.

Kezzy showed us our room right after "coffee." Pledges all had to share the same room and this one wasn't bad, just a typical dorm room with bunk beds, desks, a TV. But, "Once you've passed your tests during Pledge Week," Kezzy told us, "you each get your own room, a room like mine," and then the Pam-Anderson-looking 'ho showed us *her* room...

"Wow!" Mercy exclaimed.

"It's *beautiful!*" Hannah said.

But I was speechless. Kezzy's crib looked like a smaller version of the Presidential Suite at the Mayflower. She had a *round* bed with a mirrored ceiling, a vanity that could've been Queen Elizabeth's, the highest-class furniture, even her own fucking sauna. The haughty bitch pushed a button, then the entire wall opened up to reveal the entertainment system, the centerpiece of which was a 100-inch plasma TV. Shit, I didn't even know they *made* them that big. After a minute of gawping, I finally said, "This is the coolest room I've ever seen..."

Kezzy's high-heels took her across the shag carpet where something seemed to catch her eye. All of a sudden she looked distracted.

It was an oil painting she was looking at. I mean, it had obviously been there since the day she moved into the room but the way she was looking at it, you'd think it was Mercy looking at a painting of Jesus. What's the word? Reverence! That's it. Kezzy was looking at this old oil painting with *reverence* in her eyes.

Weirdest thing was, the painting itself. It was just an old shack on a hill with straggly open fields around it. Nighttime. A full moon in the sky.

"What's with the painting of the old shack, Miss Kezzy?" I asked.

"It's more than a shack," she snipped sternly, but when she turned, I saw a tear in her eye. "It's something very near and dear to me, and it'll be near and dear to you...if you've got what it takes to be an Alpha Sister."

I didn't know *what* she was talking about, but I didn't push it, either, 'cos I could tell it was a touchy subject. All I could think was, *It's just a fuckin' shack. Why have a gorgeous pad like this and hang a picture like THAT in it?*

"Oh, Miss Kezzy? What's this?" Hannah asked, pointing to a much smaller picture frame on the back of the door. "It looks real old."

"It is indeed, very old, Hannah," the Senior Sister said. "It's a very old and very important document, and I'd like all three of you to look at it now."

We approached the door, squinting. Like she said, it wasn't another painting, it was a document, yellowed with age. Big handwriting read:

Transfer Of Land Title & Deed

Witnesseth:

On this 30th Daye of Aprill, in ye Yeare 1750, I, Micah Whatley, do hereby grant to my deare Friend & Confidante,

Going Monstering

Mr. Joseph Curwen, of Stamper's Hill in the Rhode Island Colony, one hundred Hectares of my Land in the East Region, commencing at ye Glenn know'n as ye Cold Spring Glenn & extending to ye stone Fence of ye Roade know'n as ye Aylesbury Roade, in ye Towne of Dunwich, formerly know'n as New Dunnich, in the Colony of Massachusetts.

> **Sighed,**
> **Micah Whatley**
> **Joseph Curwen**
> **Witness: Elmer Frye, Recorder of Deeds**

"An old land deed or something," I said.

"What land?" Hannah asked.

Mercy just looked at it, her nose scrinching like at a stink.

"Who knows what a hectare is?" Kezzy asked.

None of us knew.

"Such a *bright* group of pledges this time." Kezzy smirked. "It's how they measure land sections in England, and most of Europe now, actually. But in England, they've measured land in hectares since just after the time of the Romans."

"But this says Massachusetts," Mercy whined. "That's not England."

"That's very astute of you, Mercy. You should be on Jeopardy," Kezzy laid on the sarcasm. "But in 1750 what country owned the colonies?"

"England," I said.

"I knew that!" Hannah said.

"No, you didn't, you dim, dim bulb," Kezzy kept on. "A hectare equals about 240 acres, and in that deed a man named Micah Whatley legally gave 100 hectares of his land to a friend of his named Joseph Curwen. Now, girls, why might this be important to you?"

Hannah raised her finger. "Because...," then she sighed. "I

don't know!"

"Well, the college is named Dunwich," I took a stab, "and that same name is on the deed, so I guess those 100 hectares that Whatley gave to this man Curwen wound up being some of the land this college was built on."

"Very good, Ann! Not only are you the fattest pledge this year, but evidently the smartest!"

I really appreciated that.

"Dunwich College was actually *founded* by Joseph Curwen, shortly thereafter, with an endowment he'd amassed specifically for that purpose, and his friend gave him the land on which the campus was later built," Kezzy explained. "You'll learn more as Pledge Week proceeds. Now, for the next five minutes, I'd like you girls to read that deed over and over again, at the same time contemplating its importance. While you're doing that, I'll tend to a momentary private matter."

Of all the silly *shit*. I expected her to leave the room, for whatever "private matter" she had to do but when I looked over my shoulder, I saw her standing at the other side of the room, staring up at that old painting of the shack.

"Ann?" she said without seeing that I was looking at her. "Do you have a problem comprehending instructions from the Senior Sorority Sister?"

"No, Miss Kezzy."

"Then why are you looking over your shoulder at me when I *just* instructed you to look at the document? Hmm?"

Cunt. "Sorry, Miss Kezzy." I kept my face pointed at the dumb-ass document. Re-read it to myself a couple of times, then just waited. But when I glanced to the right to admire that dynamite vanity, I caught the reflection of Kezzy's back, and when what I was seeing registered, I almost had to put my hand in my mouth to keep from laughing...

Kezzy was *playing* with herself. I'm *not* making this up. She was standing there with her feet apart, looking up at that ridiculous shack painting, and she had her skirt up and her panties pulled down. The motion of her right elbow left no doubt. She kept whispering to herself, "Fuck, fuck, oh, yeah... Fuck," like that, then she goes up on her tiptoes, arches her back, and mutters, "Shit, fuck, oooooo..."

I just shook my head. I could understand if she'd been looking at a picture of Brad Pitt. But...an old shack?

Crazy...

"Now go unpack," Kezzy said when she turned with a flushed face, "choose your bunks, and get more acquainted. Dinner's at seven. One thing you'll like — and I mean you, Ann, and Hannah, in particular — is that we serve *fabulous* meals here at Alpha House. Tonight, for example, Zenas will be serving two-pound New Zealand lobster tails."

The lobster tails sounded great, but I *had* to smirk. "Miss Kezzy? I presume that when you said Hannah and I *in particular*...you meant that because we're *fat?*"

Her flushed expression didn't change. "You *presume* quite correctly, Ann. Am I detecting a touch of the smartass? Hmm? Fat and dejected is one thing, but there's really little that's less commendable than a fat, dejected *smartass*." Her perfect fuckin' teeth sparkled at me. "Please keep that in mind. And, now, girls? Be on your way. If you must know, it's wearisome for a high-spirit like me to be in the presence of three exceedingly *low* auras such as yourselves for any length of time." She batted her long lashes. "No offense."

Oh! None taken! I thought.

We went back to our room and stowed our stuff.

"How do you like that Barbie Doll battle ax?" I gruffed when the door was closed. "I *hate* girls with implants. It turns their personalities to shit."

"Jesus! Did you hear what she said about us?" Hannah whined.

Mercy looked shocked. "Why did you have to say *Jesus?*"

"Shut up, Mercy," I said. "Sure, it's tough taking the shit she flings, but remember — during Pledge Week, that's the way it goes. If we don't like it, we can lump it. And I *can't* lump it. I *have* to do this."

"We all do," Mercy piped.

"Basically, all this is a week's worth of pranks. We can hack *that*, can't we?"

"Drinking coffee with *cum* in it is just a prank?" Hannah complained.

"Well, yeah, that *was* a little over the top..."

"It tasted *awful!*" Mercy made a face that looked like a Gumby doll in a vise. "I almost upchucked."

Great... We started unpacking but I heard voices in the hall, so I cracked the door and we all peeked outside. Zenas, in his maid's suit, was walking toward the stairs with Kezzy, and in that smooth and very appealing New England accent, he said, "Shee-it, Kezzy. Which dog pound yew get them three from?" but he pronounced "dog pound" as *dog pee-aound*. "En't seen me a uglier crew, thet's for shuh. Even wuss than last yeer."

"He's so mean!" Hannah whispered after I closed the door.

"Dog pound?" Mercy questioned. "What's he mean by that?"

"It means we're *dogs*, Mercy," I informed her. How she could have a C average in high school and still be that dumb, I couldn't tell you. "It means we're ugly."

"Yeah, well, he can go to heck!"

"It's weird, though," I told them, putting my stuff in a dresser. "Alpha House had three pledges last year, and I met them all, talked to them during orientation. In fact, they're the ones who told me about the sorority in the first place. And guess what? None of them were dogs. They were all hotties like Kezzy."

"But didn't he just say that we're uglier than the ones from last year?" Hannah asked.

"That's what it sounded like to me."

"And what was the fuss about that old silly document on the wall?" Mercy asked next.

Just an old land deed. "Who knows?" I didn't even bother to tell them I'd seen Kezzy playing with herself while she was staring at the even sillier shack painting. Who would believe it?

We flipped coins and I lost — I *always* lose things like that — so I got stuck with the top bunk. I just sat up there awhile, staring at the wall and wondering what the fuck I'd done with my life...

Around seven, Zenas barged in, chest bulging in the frilly bodice.

"Thanks for knocking," I said.

"Daon't get smurt, fattie," he said.

"You mean *smart?* Is that what you said? I thought you said *smurt.*"

The tough redneck face eyeballed me. "I'd wutch thet if'n I was yew," and then he rubbed his junk. "I jess might have ta bust yew're cherry. Then yew'd be aout."

"So the virgin thing *isn't* a sham?" I asked. "It's for real?"

"Fuh reel, aw right, and if'n yew girlies're lyin', Kezzy'll personally throw you aout the haouse."

The other girls stared at this freak in sheer horror, but I said, "What do you want, *Zeena?*"

The room turned dead silent.

"It's time fuh dinner, but fust..." The big hands on those gorgeous muscular arms shot upward, grabbed me under the armpits, and next thing I knew, I was on my knees right before him, and he'd already pulled down the pantyhose to get his cock out.

"Yew ast whut I want? How's abaout a blowjob?"

I looked, first, at his fat cock, then up at his face. "You're shitting me, right? I'd rather hang myself than blow a redneck in a maid's suit."

"Aw, thet's tew bad, fattie," and then he started putting his junk back.

"Wait, wait, wait, wait!" I blurted. "Are you implying that if I *don't* blow you, I'll get kicked out of Alpha House?"

"Mebbe, mebbe not. But whut'jew gotta understand is Kezzy caounts on me fuh my input. I could put in a good wurd fuh ya, or's a bad wurd."

24

"So you're *blackmailing* me to suck your dick?"

"New, jus givin' ya a choice," but he pronounced "choice" as *churce,* the hayseed. "Curn't *make* ya dew it. Hail, that'd be sum kind'a rape, I 'spose. Whut I'se reely dewin', though, is dewin' yew a favor."

"A favor!" I yelled. "By letting me blow you?"

"Ee-yuh. See what Kezzy durn't like is gals with sass, and gals with lotta sass ken git theerselfs kicked aout'a heer a right fast. But what I'se larn't in my time is a cock in a chick's maouth is the *best* way tew tamp down her sass."

"Oh, bullshit! You just want head!"

"Wal... Thet tew. But a'curse, it's *yew're* decision..."

My shoulders couldn't have slumped lower. I just pulled the asshole's pantyhose back down, stuffed his dick in my mouth, and started sucking. It got big quick; in fact, the damn thing was so *fat* I could barely get my lips around it, and it didn't help that the dude'd been sweating in those pantyhose all day, either.

Dick-stink, you know?

Then the rude bastard actually grabbed my ears and started pumping his hips. How romantic. "Ee-yuh, ee-yuh, thet's a good li'l fattie," he grunted, and then, "Boo-yaa!" The shit fired right down my throat so hard I thought it'd go in my fuckin' epiglottis or whatever it's called. Best way to keep from choking was to just swallow as fast as I could, so that's what I did. When he was done, he pushed my face off, and I swear when his dick came out of my mouth, it made a sound like a cork coming out of a bottle.

I fell back against the edge of the lower bunk. He patted my head and said, "Yew suck like a champ, fattie."

"Oh, thanks very much. That's a *very nice* thing to say..."

He clapped his hands. "Come on, losers! Time fuh dinner!"

We filed out after him, and all I could think about now was that big two-pound lobster tail waiting for me. Thinking about it took my mind off the gruesome fact that I now had *two* of Zenas' loads in my stomach. But just then he looked back at me and said, "And it's a good thing yew swallowed, Ann." Needless to say, he pronounced the word "swallowed" as *swallered*. We headed down the beautiful curved staircase. "See, theer en't no spittin' heer et Alpha Haouse. But...Kezzy'll 'splain the rest'a thet tew yawl later."

Me, Hannah, and Mercy all looked at each other.

"What the hell does that mean?" Hannah said.

"Yuh-yuh...yeah?" Mercy said.

"Hey, Zenas!" I called ahead. "What did you mean by that? Kezzy'll explain *what* later?"

But Zenas just laughed and led us into the dining room.

Hindsight gave me a pretty good clue what he meant. I'd heard about this girl at USC last year who had to swallow the cum of, like, fifty guys as part of her sorority hazing. The guys all jerked off in a teflon sauce pan, and that poor stupid bitch drank it all, then had to have her stomach pumped at the hospital. Would love to have seen the look on the doctor's face who did *that* job. None of us really *said* anything about Zenas's remark, but I think we all knew deep-down that we'd have to suck a *lot* of dicks if we wanted to make it through Pledge Week.

The dining room looked fit for a king's banquet. Twenty-foot-long table, silk napkins, *gold* knives, spoons, and forks, Sterling dinner plates. Another crystal chandelier overhead. Fuck. This house had *money*. Mercy and Hannah sat down but before I could, Kezzy's voice called out from the hall behind us.

"Zenas! Have Ann come in here a minute, please."

Zenas shot his thumb toward the hall. "Yew heerd her, fattie. The powder room, just off the foyer."

Now what the fuck is THIS all about? I wondered and went to the foyer. I saw a door open a few inches, and Kezzy's hand shot out, and her finger pointed, then curled inward.

"Here, Ann."

I walked in. "What the—"

"Hello, Ann," Kezzy said. "Are you and the others properly settled in your room?"

I just kind of stood there gaping, when I answered, "Yes, Miss Kezzy," because the floozy was sitting on the toilet right there in front of me with her skirt jacked up and her panties down to her ankles. Her back was arched and her chest was thrust forward. She grunted daintily and—

plip!

I saw a little turd hit the toilet water in the V between her legs.

"Pardon me a moment, Ann. I'm defecating."

"I can see that!"

"And don't be uncomfortable. After all, we are both women, aren't we?"

I nodded, kind of numb. Her pussy, by the way, was shaved bald. And, as I might have expected, it was a *perfect* pussy...

"There is, however, a transitive *reason* why I happen to be defecating while giving you the opportunity to witness it," she said, and then she relaxed and—

"Ahhhhh...."

—began to pee.

"You see, I'm testing your powers of observation." The stream of tinkle dribbled down. "Now, watch very carefully, and—please—be observant." She stood up, pulled her panties back up and her skirt back down, flushed the toilet, washed her hands in the marble-basined sink, then said, "Come along," and took me back to the dining room.

Immediately, I thought, *What finishing school did YOU go to? You forgot to wipe your ass!*

"Hello, girls," she greeted. "I trust you're all settled and find your room satisfactory?"

"Yes, Miss Kezzy," Hannah and Mercy said.

I started to move off but Kezzy stopped me. "Don't sit down just yet, Ann." Then she turned right to me, unbuttoned her blouse, and pulled her boobs out.

The room went dead-silent, just like upstairs.

See, Kezzy's boobs were the kind that just about any girl

would *sell their soul* to have. They were perfect 38DD's, with just as perfect medium-pink nipples big around as silver dollars.

She walked to the end of the table where Hannah and Mercy sat. "Girls?" she said. "I'd like each of you to take a moment and feel my breasts," and she leaned them over toward Hannah. Hannah's eyes went wide; she hesitated, and then eventually touched Kezzy's boobs.

"Don't be bashful, Hannah. Squeeze them." She chuckled. "And you needn't worry. I'm not a lesbian."

Hannah squeezed them a few times, still tongue-tied, and then Kezzy put them right up to Mercy.

"Go on, Mercy. I assure you, this isn't a sexual thing, so there's no reason to fret about Christian sin. I'm merely initiating an exercise of observation, the reason of which will be revealed momentarily."

"I-I-I," Mercy blabbered, then she squeezed her eyes shut and felt Kezzy's tits.

"Good, good." Kezzy's smile beamed when she walked right up to me, boobs out-thrust. "Feel my breasts, Ann."

I did what she said but was already feeling a little sick.

"There. Now." Kezzy redid her blouse, crossed her arms, and began tapping her foot in that irritating way she always did. "Observation lends itself toward experience — *tactile* observation just as much as visual observation. During the time each of you were feeling my absolutely beautiful breasts, did any of you receive the impression that they were *implants?*"

Mercy and Hannah shook their heads in silence. Then Kezzy's smile collapsed and turned back into that Napoleon-bust grimace. "Earlier, our friend Ann here made the remark that she '*hates* girls with implants.' Ann, who were you referring to, since you now know beyond a doubt that my breasts are one-hundred-percent natural? Hmm?"

Then I got the gist, like that, like a light switch, and that's why I suddenly wanted to throw up. My voice sounded like rocks being ground together when I said, "You've got a bug in our room, don't you?"

"Why, of course, you silly, drab, dour, overweight thing, you. We have tiny microphones all over Alpha House, and each and every one of them is turned on during Pledge Week." She pulled her panties down and her skirt up. "Ah, but as the old adage goes: the best way to learn is the *hard* way. Yes?" and then she leaned over the table. "Ann? The 'Barbie Doll battle ax' wants you to lick her ass." She spread her butt cheeks wide.

My knees were wobbling. "But, but...you didn't...wipe..."

"Very good! You're observant after all! No, I deliberately did *not* wipe myself after defecating, Ann, because, as punishment for your bad attitude, your obstinance, and your shameful be-hind-my-back insults, *you* will wipe for me. With your tongue."

I stared at her ass. It was perfect, just like her boobs and pussy, the kind of ass I'd do anything to have but knew I never *would* have. No matter how much weight I lost, how much ex-ercise, whatever. Bad genes versus great genes, I guess. Kezzy had the best body I'd ever seen on a woman, period. I envied it, and I guess that just made me hate her more. Great body, sure, but she was a shitty person, so that had to count for *something*, right?

All in all, though, it didn't matter how great her ass *looked*. She had *shit* in her crack right now, and if I wanted to stay in Alpha House...

I had to lick it.

"Well, Ann? Just how badly do you want to be an Alpha Sister?"

I got down on my knees. *Holy, holy shit...*

Hannah looked petrified, but it was Mercy who piped up, "Don't do it, Ann! Don't let Miss Kezzy manipulate you like that! It isn't right!"

"Really, Mercy?" Kezzy said. "I think I'm being quite a gen-erous sport about this. In the past, any Pledge with the audac-ity to *insult* the Senior Sorority Sister has been immediately ex-pelled from the house. I *could* do that, but I'm not. Ann, do you

Going Monstering

believe you should be punished for your insults?"

I had no choice but to answer, "Yes, Miss Kezzy."

"But it's demeaning!" Mercy harped. "Don't do it, Ann! It's not the end of the world if you don't get into Alpha House!"

I just kept staring at her butt-crack. I could see some brown in there...

"I'm glad you said that, Mercy," Kezzy remarked, still bent over the table. "I believe that Ann *will* do it, because—*unlike* you—she has resolve. She has set a goal for herself, and that goal is to become an esteemed Alpha House Sister, and she will do anything necessary to achieve that goal. Of course, there are very rare occasions when I'm wrong. If Ann decides right this very minute to get up, put her things back in her suitcase, and leave this house...then you, Mercy, will lick my ass in her stead."

"Do it, Ann!" Mercy railed. "Don't be a sissy. Just do it and get it over with!"

"You're so predictable, Mercy," Kezzy chuckled.

Fuckin' Mercy. But Kezzy—correction, *fuckin'* Kezzy—was right. A second later, my face was stuck right up her unwiped butt, my tongue wagging away. That smear of poop over her butt-hole came off on the first lick, and let me tell you—it's a taste that takes a long time to go away. I tried to breathe through my mouth but that only worked part way. After a few more licks I just said fuck it, and lapped her asshole like a dog licking its master's face.

"Good, good, Ann. That feels quite nice. Five more minutes will be sufficient."

When you're licking ass, five minutes seems like five hours. Ever try eating ass? Don't. Oh, and get this. The bitch was fingering her clit while I was doing it, and she even had the balls to reach around with one hand and push the back of my head to get my mouth tighter. Then she kind of tensed up, stamped a foot, and got off. She even squealed. When she said, "That's enough now, Ann. Your punishment has been dispensed," I jumped up and ran to the powder room. I washed my face and lips with the bar of soap, then I even *sucked* the bar to try and get the taste out. *Two-pound lobster tail,* I kept thinking. At least I had *something* to look forward to. But even with the soap-taste in my mouth, I could still taste a ghost of her shit.

"What the hell's this?" I demanded when I got back to the dining room. Kezzy and Zenas were cutting into their giant, broiled lobster tails and dipping the chunks in drawn butter, but Hannah and Mercy were dragging their spoons through these little plastic cups. There was an identical cup on my plate. "This looks like yogurt!"

"It is, Ann. The store-brand kind," Kezzy said and ate another chunk of butter-dipped lobster.

"That's fucked up! You said we were having lobster tails!" I yelled.

"Ann? It's uncouth to raise your voice at the table," Kezzy chided me. "And, yes, I did say, precisely, that Zenas would be serving two-pound lobster tails tonight. But I *never* said he'd be serving them to *you.*" She huffed a laugh. "You girls are *pledges,* for goodness sake. You'll get your lobster tails when you pass initiation."

Another rip-off. I was so pissed I thought my head would explode. You don't fuck with fat people like that. Fuckin' *yogurt.* I *hate* yogurt. *Yogurt* is boring. By then I was too pissed off and humiliated to care, so I just stirred the slop around and ate it. Oh, and it was the unflavored kind. Dynamite. We spent the next twenty minutes watching Zenas and Kezzy eat their gorgeous lobster tails.

But it was Kezzy herself who brought out dessert. She and Zenas each had a giant piece of triple-layer chocolate cake. Hannah and Mercy each got one M&M. But me?

I fumed. "Where's *my* dessert, Miss Kezzy?"

"You had *your* dessert early, Ann." She grinned and forked into her cake. "My ass."

Going Monstering

☠ ☠ ☠

A HALF-HOUR after dinner, Zenas led us back up the stairs, but once we were on the landing he turned us away from our room. He took us down the opposite hall, and into—

"Wait, a minute," I asked, as confused as Hannah and Mercy. "What kind of room is this?"

Bright white lights shined down on the tile floor.

"It's the exam suite," came a cultured voice from behind an opened door in the back.

"We have to take *exams?*" Hannah whined.

Mercy whined right with her. "The semester doesn't start for another week!"

I kind of groaned out my suspicion. "I don't think it's that kind of exam..."

"Get aout'a them duds'n put these heer things on," Zenas said and shoved some white smocks at us.

Fuck, I thought. *These people aren't fooling around.* That fucker Zenas just stood there watching us as we took off our clothes, and when I got mine off, he laughed and said, "Wal, gawd-*durn*, girl! Thet's some serious fat yew're packin' and"—his jaw dropped when I took my blouse and bra off. My breasts kind of just dropped out. "Them theer's the *wust* pair'a tits I evuh seen! Look like two white socks with tennis balls in the end."

"Thanks a lot," I muttered, but he was right; my boobs sucked. His eyes tracked over to Hannah who feebly stepped out of her clothes. "Et least thet'n theer's got a pair a fella wouldn't might suckin' on in a pinch, but—shee-it!—didn't *know* gals had feet *thet* big!" I don't think Hannah heard the insult 'cos she was crying, just like Mercy, who took the longest to strip. When she had her top off, Zenas whistled. "I guess some gals juss wurn't born with tits. 'Cos I shuh durn't seen none on yew."

32

Edward Lee

"Do you have to stand here and watch!" she blubbered.

"sure dew, string bean. Got's ta make sure everythin' goes right," he chuckled, "but I'll tell ya's sumpthin'. I best not watch *tew* long 'cos yew girls're so *fuggin'* UGLY, I might not be able ta get wood for a yeer."

"Why is he making us *do* this!" Mercy bawled like a baby.

"They're gonna examine us," I'd already put two and two together, "to make sure we're really virgins."

"You mean, you mean...*examine* us? Our, our, our—"

"Our *vaginas*, bonehead. To check and see if we still have hymens."

"Yes, yes, young lady," that refined voice returned, but this time an old country doctor walked out of the back office in a white labcoat. He looked over circular spectacles at a clipboard. "And you must be...Miss Ann White. Girls, I'm Dr. Willet, and I'm the Alpha House physician on call. As Ann here has so accurately deduced, I'll be performing your gynecological exams. Though I think I can safely say through the most cursory visual assessment that the three of you are in all likelihood, *chaste.*"

Mercy shot a desperate glance to me. "What, what's he *mean?*"

I put my white smock on which, naturally, was several sizes too small so I looked like I was busting out of it. "It means were' so fuckin' *unattractive* that no guy in a million years would ever want to put his dick in our vaginas."

"A bit coarsely stated," the doctor said, "but essentially correct."

When Mercy pulled her panties off, Zenas bent over at the waist he was laughing so hard. See, Hannah and I kept ourselves reasonably trimmed down there, but Mercy clearly hadn't trimmed her plot, like, *ever.* She had *so much hair* between her legs, it looked liked one of those black Halloween wigs.

Zenas was honking like a horn. "Thet yew're pussy har, girl, or yew gotta hedgehog 'tween yer gams?" Meanwhile, this shrivel-faced Dr. Willet reached under each exam table and—

clack! — pulled up stirrups. "As they say in the military, young ladies...assume the position."

I just resigned to the whole thing and got on, put my heels in the stirrups, and waited. Mercy and Hannah looked like they were about to have fuckin' strokes when they got on. Then that old prune-faced fuck Dr. Willet put this thing on his head that looked like the things jewelers used to examine gems, with a little light on it, and he had a pair of stainless-steel retractors in his hand. "Ah, now — yes," he said and pulled a rolling chair right up between Hannah's legs. "Um-hmm, um-hmm," he muttered, nodded, then wheeled over to Mercy who was still crying and vibrating like she was being fuckin' electrocuted. "I must say, Mercy, yours is a case of pubic hirsutism unlike any that I've witnessed in nearly sixty years of practicing medicine."

"*Huh?*" she whined.

"It means you've got the *hairiest pussy* he's ever seen!" I yelled to her.

"Oh..."

Then he wheeled over to me, took his peek, and stood up. "Well, girls, I'm happy to say that there are no prevaricators among you. You are all, incontestably, virgins."

"Great, doc," I said. "Can we go now?"

"Not just yet, Ann. You see, being the sorority's physician on call, I am entitled to a privilege or two. But it will only take a minute," and then the old fuck opened his pants.

"You've got to be shitting me," I muttered.

He pointed to Hannah, said, "Eeeny," then to Mercy, "Meeny," then to me, "Miney," but when his finger was half-way back to Hannah, it shot right back to me.

"Moe."

"Oh, come on, man!" I yelled. "That's unfair as shit!"

"I'd prefer the word 'untoward,' but, yes, I suppose it is." He grinned, showing dentures. "I'm afraid there's just something about you, Ann."

"What? I gotta *blow you?* Gimme a break; you can't get it up!

You've got to be *eighty!*"

"I'm eighty-six, actually, Ann, but I'm in tip-top condition. Why, I'd wager my blood-pressure is lower than yours." He pulled his dick out of his shorts and, of course, it was hard and big. Then he took out a tube of vaseline and put a big blob of it on his knob. "But you may rest easy. Fellatio is not my intention at all. I'd much prefer *penetration*, and you needn't worry about my putting your virginity in jeopardy. You see, and as they called it in the old days, the *nether-orifice* is much more to my liking."

"Terrific," I said.

"Nether-*what?*" Mercy bawled.

"He gonna fuck her in the *ass*," Hannah whispered.

Dr. Willet stepped right up, pulled my cheeks apart, and slid that eighty-six-year-old hard-on right in. I'd done it enough times that it was no big deal anymore, and it never hurt. You just kind of relax and push out a little. But this old fuck hadn't even stroked one time before he looked at me over his spectacles and said, "Why, Ann, I see that *your* anus is certainly no stranger to the admission of a penis on occasion..."

"Maybe fifty or sixty, if you gotta know."

"Splendid! I simply adore a truly *seasoned* woman," and then the old crank wrapped his arms around my thighs and started banging away. Hannah and Mercy were both sitting up on their tables, watching through their fingers, and Zenas just stood there rubbing his crotch grinning with that big redneck white-trash shuck-and-jive backwoods grin.

It took the doc, like, fifteen fuckin' minutes to come, and by then my butt felt like a butter-churner. "Ah," he said, and, "Mmm," and then I could feel it squirting up my rear. Then just like that, he wiped his dick off on my smock, zipped up, and said, "Thank you, Ann. And to all of you, you have my very best wishes!" Then he went back into his office.

High heels ticked across the floor; it was Kezzy who'd just waltzed in, that fake smile lighting up the room. "Congratulations, girls. The three of you have just passed your first day of initiation as Alpha House pledges. You may do whatever you like with the remainder of the evening."

💀 💀 💀

WELL, the first thing *I* did with the remainder of the evening was run to the bathroom and shit that codger's cum out of my ass. Just knowing it was there bothered the hell out of me, and it bothered me even more knowing that I also had not one but two samples of Zenas's cum in my stomach. When I was done sitting on the bowl, I turned right around, rammed my finger down my throat, and got *that* out of me, too. It was mostly that yogurt that came up, but I knew Zenas's jizz was in there somewhere, so at least I felt a little better. Then I turned on the shower but—

No water came out.

For *fuck's sake!* The sink worked and the toilet flushed, but the shower was a no-go. So I washed up, went back into the dorm room, and put on my nightgown. Hannah and Mercy were both asleep, but they were both kind of quivering under the covers, like they were having bad dreams.

Can't say that I blamed them.

In the hall, I saw that only a few lights were on downstairs, but it wasn't even past nine o'clock so I didn't see any harm in knocking on Kezzy's—correction, *fuckin'* Kezzy's— door. I wanted to take a shower, damn it, and it was ridiculous to think that the showers could be broken in a decked-out house like this. But when I knocked...

No answer.

I opened the door a crack. "Miss Kezzy? Sorry to bother you but our shower's not working..."

No reply.

I looked in then, and all the lights were out. She wasn't in bed. *Probably boffing that scumbag Zenas, the bitch.* The last door before the stairs read ALPHA HOUSE LIBRARY. *Maybe she's in there*, but when I tried the door, the fucker was locked.

Not a sound downstairs. I milled around the dining room, living room, checked the laundry room, the kitchen, but Kezzy wasn't to be found. There was a big-ass quadruple-door fridge like they have in restaurants, and I thought a second about peeking in and grabbing something but didn't. *That 'ho's got hidden microphones all over, so she's probably got hidden cameras, too.* I was fuckin' *starving* but I knew my luck, which was always bad. If I even opened that door, she'd know, and I'd either get kicked out for stealing or have to lick her ass again. No thanks.

I caught a glimpse of another door in the kitchen corner, with window panes. I looked outside and saw the backyard. Like the inside, the outside was something to write home about. A courtyard, fieldstone paths, a gurgling fountain with underwater lights, flowerbeds all around. There were no other lights except the ones in the fountain, but the door was unlocked so I figured it'd be okay to step outside. *No one said I couldn't,* I reasoned. I wandered around in the moonlight for a while, and it was really creepy how *still* everything felt. I followed some hedgerows past the flowerbeds, and when I peeked around —

There she is!

The backyard was longer than I'd thought, and past the hedges and flowerbed was a gazebo built near the high brick wall that bordered the property. Only a tiny candle was burning, and there, at a table, sat Kezzy, reading a book. But that wasn't the first thing I'd noticed.

The *first* thing was that Kezzy was stark-friggin' naked.

Kid you not. There was the prim and proper Senior Sorority Sister without a stitch on, reading this book. All I could tell was it looked like an *old* book, and bigger than most. I didn't want to say anything — like about the shower — 'cos the whole scene was a bad vibe. After a minute, though, she closed the book, leaned back in the chair, and put her feet up on the table-edge.

Then she started playing with herself.

I don't fuckin' believe this! I thought.

Her head was back with this dreamy look on her face. I stood there a while and looked at her — jealous as shit. Her body was so beautiful. I'd already seen her play with herself twice today — once, mind you, with my face stuck between her ass-cheeks — so this was something I could do without. She was murmuring while she was doing it, but I couldn't hear the words. *Fuck this*, I thought, and went back inside. I figured I'd just go upstairs and go to bed, and try not to think what tomorrow might bring. But something stopped me when I was halfway across the living room...

Hanging over the mantle of the giant stone fireplace was a big portrait. There were a bunch of paintings in the house — most of them old — but I hadn't really looked at any of them except for that painting of the ridiculous old shack in Kezzy's room. I turned on a lamp and stared up at this one, though, 'cos all of a sudden something seemed captivating about it.

It was a painting of some fussy-looking guy with a pointed goatee, wearing a cloak with a flapped up collar. Under his arm was a big book with metal hinges. The book looked damaged, beat up, with tan leather that was all scuffed. *Just some dude from a long time ago*, I thought, but then I noticed a little brass name-plate on the bottom of the frame. It read:

Joseph Corwan, Esquire & Gentleman
of the Colony of Rhode Island.
b. February 28, 1662
d. April 12, 1711

Could this be..., I started to think, but then, *No.* The name of the guy who founded the college was Joseph Curwen. Curwen and Corwan were similar, but it had to be a coincidence 'cos according to the land deed upstairs, Joseph *Curwen* took ownership of the land in 1750, almost forty years after this Corwan guy kicked off..

No big deal, but—

Something nagged at me now. *The nameplate?* I'm not the most observant girl in the world but I did observe this: the painting was obviously real old, and so was the frame, but that nameplate looked brand-new. I squinted at it and an indentation around the plate—an indentation in the frame's wood—almost as if an original plate had been removed and this new plate had been screwed into its place, only the new plate was a tiny bit smaller.

Hmm, I thought. But why would I care? Why would I even notice this?

From the kitchen, I heard the door to the backyard click open, so I switched off the light and scooted back upstairs. It had to have been Kezzy, and I didn't want to explain why I was gaping at this old painting; plus, I didn't really want to see her naked again 'cos her body just burned me up. She got born with that, and I got born with *this*. What a ripoff.

When I got back inside my room, though, I kept the door opened a crack...

Couple minutes later, here comes Kezzy, nude as suspected, and with that book under her arm. She unlocked the door to the library, went inside, then came back out and relocked it. Then she went to her room and that was that.

Weird shit...

I fell asleep fast but had some real dog-shit dreams. First I dreamed that that dude in the painting, Corwan, was jerking off in my face but when he came, I could *see* his cum landing on me but I couldn't *feel* it. I was paralyzed in the dream, and all I could do was lie there with my mouth cranked open, while this guy shot his dream-load right in my mouth. Fuck. Then Corwan disappears like a ghost, and guess who's standing there a little later?

Zenas. Only he's not wearing the maid get-up now, he's wearing a ballerina suit, the tutu, the little slippers, that deal. I try to yell, "You look ridiculous!" but I can't 'cos I'm still paralyzed, so then the asshole blows his nose in his hand and smears it into my mouth. "Ee-yuh," he chuckles, "thar's some redneck marmalade fuh ya, fattie." Yeah, what a sport, huh? Of course, I can't blame Zenas 'cos it was *my* subconscious mind that created the shit. Anyway, after that the dream turns black, and I'm just lying there for what feels like hours and hours, until it occurred to me that I must be dead, but sometime later, the blackness fades and it's Kezzy climbing onto the bed. She squats very daintily over my head, then plants her twat right on my mouth. "Get me off," she whispers, so I start eating her out, and though I've never done anything like that before in real life, I'm kind of liking it in the dream, and I'm kind of liking her, too, which makes absolutely no sense. She starts twitching and then comes in my face, whispering, "That's lovely, that's lovely," and then a snake shoots out of her pussy and goes right down my throat so far I can feel it wriggling around in my stomach.

After that I thought I woke up, but I know I must've still been dreaming, because the darkness in the room is real grainy and it's actually *moving*, and I hear these words, or at least *thought* I did 'cos they were really low, and the words are kind of moving too, just like the darkness. The words, gibberish, sounded something like this: "Shub neb hyr'ik eb hyr'k. Ogthrod ai'f geb'l, ee'h yog-sothoth," over and over and over for hours and hours, and I'm *sure* it was Kezzy's voice speaking the gibberish.

I woke up to the sound of the highest-pitched scream I've ever heard, and I started screaming myself and so did Mercy and Hannah, and then the lights snapped on. Thought my heart was gonna pop, but then I looked over my top bunk and saw Zenas—correction, *fuckin'* Zenas—standing there in his maid's suit.

"You DICK!" I yelled.

It was no one *screaming*; it was that dickbrain blowing a fucking referee's whistle.

"Rise'n shine, girlies!" he cracked, but the rube pronounced "shine" as *shan*. "Git'chewer tired asses up'n aout!"

I looked at the clock on the desk and saw that it was 6 a.m. Zenas threw a pair of these ludicrous cotton-candy-pink sweats on each of our bunks. "Yew got five minutes to be aoutside in back!" then he walked out.

"That fucker," I mumbled. I climbed down and saw that Hannah was still shivering from the shock of that whistle, and Mercy — the little wuss — was actually crying.

"Why did he *do* that?" she blubbered.

"'Cos he's a dick in a maid's suit, and we've still got a week of hazing," I told her.

"Five minutes, he said?" Hannah belly-ached. "We don't even have time to take showers!"

"Wouldn't matter if we did 'cos the shower — correction, the *fuckin'* shower — is busted." I took off my nightgown, was about to step into the sweat pants, but thought, *Holy SHIT*, and then put them to my face and sniffed. "These sweats *stink!*"

Mercy took a sniff, too...then started crying again.

Anyway, we did the gig. What choice did we have? It was just more of Kezzy's twisted humiliation bullshit. Figured she was gonna make us jog up and down sorority road in stinky, hot-pink sweats so we'd be the laughing stock. Oh, and the best part?

My sweats were so many sizes too small that I looked like I'd been spray-painted.

"Good morning, pledges!" Kezzy greeted in the backyard. The haughty bitch was wearing shorts, a tube top, white Nikes with little pink sockies, and a day-glo-orange baseball cap with her perfect blond fucking ponytail sticking out the back. "Exercise time. A fit body makes a fit mind."

The stink wafting up off our sweatclothes was making us

gag. "Miss Kezzy, these sweats *fuckin' stink,* and we couldn't even wash 'cos the fuckin' showers are busted."

She walked up and pinched my nose. "Oh, you eloquent one, you. The showers aren't 'fuckin' busted,' Ann. I merely shut the water off. And, yes, your exercise apparel may well 'fuckin' stink,' but that's the idea. Countless pledges have worn those before you—pledges who passed initiation, by the way— so you can appreciate the symbology."

"Symbology!"

"Think of the sweatclothes as having been *tinctured* by the success of past pledges, and hope that their *feminine essence* will rub off on you. It's for good luck."

Great. B.O. was good luck now. But what could I do? *Nothing,* I told myself. *Just grin and bear it...and STINK.*

In the morning light, the backyard looked a lot bigger than it had last night; there were more gardens than I'd realized, and a couple more fountains. Birds were hopping around on the gazebo where Kezzy'd frigged herself off while reading the book. I hadn't noticed the giant barbeque and tennis court, either.

And I also hadn't noticed the pile of rocks.

That's right, toward the west stone fence sat a pile of *rocks,* and it was a *big* pile—I mean, like twenty feet wide and five feet high. Looked like chunks of granite.

Hannah raised a shaking hand. "Mmm-Miss Kezzy. Whuh-why is there a big pile of rocks over there?"

"Because *you* girls," Kezzy explained in a smart-ass sing-song voice, "are going to move them over *there,*" and then she pointed to all the way over to the east stone fence, where we could all see a big bald spot on the grass.

"We're not the first ones to wear these stinking clothes," I said, "and we're not the first ones to move those rocks..."

"Very perceptive," Kezzy said. "Now you best be quick about it. You don't want to be out here when it starts to get hot."

"Come on," I said to the others. "Let's not bitch about it, let's just do it," and then we all grabbed our first rock and waddled it over to the other side where we started the new pile. In *sweat-clothes?* We didn't want to move rocks in sweatclothes once it started to get hot, like, probably around 11...

It was *four fuckin' o'clock* in the afternoon by the time we finished. You probably always hear about how cold Massachusetts is in the winter, but in August? It gets hot as hell. Kezzy was sweet enough to give us temperature readings every hour; by four it was almost ninety.

We felt *dead* when we dropped the last rocks. Every muscle in my body *ached*—shit, even my *fat* ached. Hannah fell down a bunch of times, and Mercy, shit, she was crying for the last two hours. And we were *cooking* the whole time. Our cotton-candy-pink sweatclothes turned maroon real fucking fast from our sweat, and we stank so bad we had flies following us. Worst part was just *thinking* about it: *old* sweat-stink mixing with *new* sweat-stink. Shit, I was marinating. Kezzy let us go to the gazebo to get in the shade when we finished, and that's the first time I was ever *happy* to see Zenas. He was pouring us each a big-ass glass of something to drink.

"Ice-cold sweet lemonade, girls," Kezzy said. "You've worked hard today and you all deserve it." We all grabbed our glasses at the same time, took a big, welcome ice-cold chug, but then—

We *blasted* it all out of our mouths at once.

Zenas was honking laughter, and Kezzy had a giant grin on her face. It wasn't lemonade, it was straight lemon juice.

We all hit the ground on that one.

"Curn't ya take a joke?" Zenas chuckled. It was everything I could do not to kick him in the dick. He threw us each a bottle of water, and at least that wasn't fucked up.

"I'm very pleased, ladies," Kezzy said. "We don't want weaklings and fussbudgets at Alpha House, we want women who finish what they start," but when we looked over, we saw that she was standing twenty feet away.

"Miss Kezzy?" I asked, sopped in my reeking sweatclothes.

Going Monstering

"Um, why are you standing way over there?"

"Well, if you must know, Ann, I'm standing way over here because, quite frankly, you girls *stink* worse than a garbage dumpster.

"But you're the one who's making us stink!" I jumped up and yelled. "You don't let us take showers, you make us move rocks in the hot sun, and you force us to wear DIRTY FUCKIN' CLOTHES!"

"Yes, yes, I know, you poor things, but it's all part of the rigors of hazing. Get out of those malodorous sweats now, and Zenas will put them in plastic and hang them up for next year's pledges."

We all looked at each other, shrugged, and started stripping. Anything to get *out* of that hot shit. The fence was ten-feet high so it's not like anyone else could see us. Zenas actually put a clothespin on his nose when he took the stink-drenched sweat-clothes and walked them back into the house, leaving us to sit fuming, naked, hot, and humiliated.

"And, yes," Kezzy went on, "it's most regrettable that you weren't able to take showers; however, now that you've successfully completed the next phase of your initiation, I *will* allow you all to take a bath."

"But, Miss Kezzy, there isn't a bath tub in our room," I said.

She crossed her arms and kept up that superbitch grin. "You won't need a tub for *this* kind of bath, girls. You see, you'll be giving yourselves *tongue* baths."

"*What?*" Mercy whined, eyes bulging. "*What* did she say?"

Hannah put her face in her hands and just started moaning. Me? I just glared.

"Two on one, in this order," Kezzy barked out. "Mercy, Ann, and Hannah. Chop-chop, ladies. Right out here in the middle of the yard."

Hannah and I had to practically drag Mercy out of the gazebo. "*What* did she say?" she bawled.

"We have to lick each others bodies!" I snapped back.

"But, but...we're *dirty!*"

"That's why she's making us do it."

Leave it to Kezzy to think of something this sick; then the bitch added, "Arm pits first, then pussies, then butts."

Fuck. Mercy wasn't crying as much when me and Hannah started on her. I sucked one arm pit, Hannah did the other, then we put Mercy down, held our breath, and gave her a double-hummer. Try eating a girl's cooter after she's done hours of hard labor in the sun—in *sweats*—and hasn't washed in over a day. But that was a walk in the park compared to Mercy's *ass.*

I won't bother describing the fiasco, except to say it was the WORST THING TO EVER HAPPEN TO ME. I've had sweet and sour shrimp, but sweet and sour *ass?* Skip it. And you couldn't yell at the other two for smelling worse than a manure pit 'cos you knew you smelled just as bad. And I don't know *what* Hannah had eaten besides that yogurt the day before. Must've been some kind of greasy fish and asparagus maybe. Eating Kezzy's butt the night before, even with the poop smear, was fuckin' *angel food cake* compared to that. Oh, and I forgot to mention, Hannah'd started her period that morning.

While we were doing it, Kezzy and Zenas were busting their guts laughing so hard. Mercy looked like she was in shock when we were finished, and Hannah and I just stood there with smeared mouths smelling like butt-sweat. You wipe your lips off on your arm but, believe me, that don't work. My face felt so shriveled up from the sheer horror of it all, I thought it was trying to turn itself inside-out. Eventually, Kezzy dismissed us, and even though we were dead-tired from moving rocks, we all ran faster than we'd ever run and clunked upstairs.

I think we were all partially insane when we piled into the shower; I already had it in my head that if that psycho 'ho Kezzy *still* hadn't turned the water on, I was going to kill her, eat everything in the fridge, then rip off the Rolls and head for the hills. Not positive but I think I really might've done it—that's how fucked up you get when you're forced to eat dirty pussies

Going Monstering

and asses. But the water did come on and I'll bet we each used a thousand gallons of water scrubbing ourselves raw. We almost got in a fight over the Listerine, and when *that* ran out I just said fuck it and gargled with rubbing alcohol.

We laid around in our bunks, nursing our stomachaches and sore muscles. Mercy would break into these off and on crying fits, and sometimes I could hear her praying under her breath. If there *was* a God, He wasn't doing much for his servant Mercy. Hannah just laid there and moaned, and eventually she blurted, "Why is she *doing* this to us?"

"She's trying to break us, Hannah," I told her.

"Oh, no!" Mercy shrilled, "she's already done that!"

"No, she hasn't, and we can't let her!" I groaned when I sat up on my bunk. "We have to *show* her that she can't. Because if she *can*, then we go home the same three losers we were when we got here. She's like a drill sergeant in the Marines. She wants to make sure we're tough enough."

"No, no, no," Mercy kept sobbing. "It's so much more than that! It's evil..."

Hannah and I gaped at her.

"*She's*...evil."

"Bullshit, Mercy," I said. "There's no such thing as evil. Things are either fucked up or they're not, and this...is fucked up. Life has its trials, that's all. We're going to get through this, and we'll do that by sticking together as a *team*."

But she just lay there shaking her head in a daze. "No, no, it's evil. She's evil, Zenas is evil, the whole *house* is evil." She shivered. "I can *feel* it."

Whatever. Maybe she was going off the deep end; eating dirty butts can do that to a person. But later on, Kezzy called us downstairs for "dinner," which consisted of bacon-wrapped filets for Kezzy and Zenas, and a couple of salt-free pretzel rods for us. I would rather have stuck 'em up both their asses but I ate them anyway. After dinner, we were ordered to get into the Rolls.

Edward Lee

Zenas sat in the driver's seat. He was still wearing his maid's suit but now he also wore a chauffeur's hat. The *dick*. Kezzy sat up front.

"After such a hard day's work," she said in her typical phony bubbly voice, "I thought you girls would appreciate a drive through town." Then she snapped her gaze back to us. "Well, *wouldn't* you? *Wouldn't* you appreciate a drive through town?"

"Yes, Miss Kezzy," we all said at once.

"I thought so..."

She and Zenas were eating a bunch of Tastycake Butterscotch Krimpets. Those things were my favorite food when I was a kid, and they still tasted the same these days. We could *smell* them in the backseat. You could almost *taste* that delicious butterscotch icing from the smell. And they had a whole *box* of the things up front; Kezzy and Zenas were *stuffing* them into their mouths.

I leaned forward. "Um, Miss Kezzy? Do you think, maybe, we could have some of those Krimpets, please?"

She looked back with raised brow. "Well, Ann, you girls *have* partaken in some considerable toil today, and you've shown great strength and gumption. If it were up to me, I wouldn't hesitate to let you all have some Krimpets. But in the interests of equality, I'll leave the decision to Zenas." She looked over to him. "Zenas? Do you feel that the girls deserve some Krimpets?"

"Wal, now, 'tis true they worked hard today," and, of course, the redneck scumbag pronounced "worked hard" as *wucked hod*. "And, ee-yuh, they'se all of 'em passed theer virgin test, so's, yew know, to the ideer'a them desarvin' sum Krimpets, I'd have to say—"

We all crossed out fingers, and Mercy was even whispering prayers.

"—FUCK no!" Zenas cracked. "Yougurt'n pretzels is good enough fer 'em," and then he crammed another Krimpet in his mouth. He and Kezzy were *wheezing* laughter.

47

Going Monstering

Man, oh, man. The hits just kept on comin'. This really *was* sick. They were pushing our buttons like they've never *been* pushed; it was like psychological torture. You make girls drink spooged coffee and lick reeking arm pits, crotches, and ass-cracks, then dangle Krimpets in their faces and say *fuck no*. Those two fuckers laughed a while longer, like fuckin' hyenas, and we just sat back there kind of smoldering. Best way to get my mind off how much I hated them was to just look out the window at the town, but that's when I discovered that there really *was* no town. Dunwich Women's College pretty much existed in the middle of nowhere. All around were either woods or shitty looking farmland. Every now and then we'd pass some piss-ant gas station, or some rickety fruit stand, or some piss-ant shack with a bunch of piss-ant rubes sitting on the front porch. Oh, and there was a piss-ant general store that looked like it used to be a church. We saw some trailers, too, and old cars rusting in the woods; then when the woods'd change over to fields, there might be some cows grazing, and some busted tractors and half-collapsed old farmhouses. Zenas cruised the Rolls down all these long winding roads; it was kind of scenic, especially when the sun started going down. Rustic, I guess that's the word.

"See, girls, this entire area, for miles around and for years and years, used to be called Dunwich, and a great portion of this land was owned by a family that settled here in the late-1600's, the Whatley family." Kezzy turned her stone face back to us again. "Now, who's going to impress me and tell me why that name is not only familiar but important? Hannah?"

"Well, Miss Kezzy, that name's important because, because..." Then Hannah stalled, like she always did. "Oh, I don't know!"

"You're so, so bright, Hannah," Kezzy chided. "Do you happen to be missing your brain since your last bowel movement? Hmm?" She turned to me. "Ann?"

I remembered that dumb-ass deed on her wall. "Because *Mi-*

cah Whatley was the man who gave the land the college is on to another man, a friend of his, who later founded the college."

"*I really am impressed!*" and then Kezzy sneered at Mercy. "And *who* was that man who founded the college, Mercy?"

"Um, um—oh, I know! Elmer Fudd!"

"Oh, Mercy, Mercy, Mercy," Kezzy shook her head. "What *am* I going to do with you? Yours is an ignorance truly unparalleled in modern times."

"Elmer *Frye* was only the recorder of deeds for the transaction of the land," I said. "The guy who founded the college was Joseph Curwen, I think."

"You think *correct*, Ann. At least the lights aren't out in *every* house tonight. Regardless, over the decades—over the centuries, as a matter of fact—the Whatley family as well as the other families of Dunwich deteriorated, and eventually, by, say, the 1930's, all of the land *around* the college was either annexed by neighboring counties or sold off by the state. But this land—that we're driving on now?—looks *just* like it did back in the old days, the *Colonial* days, the days that provided the very foundation of this great country we live in now. It has a nice, nostalgic feel. Nostalgia is so important, don't you think?" She glared at Hannah. "Well, don't you, *Hannah?*"

"Yuh-yes, Miss Kezzy!"

"And *why?* Why, Hannah, is nostalgia so important?"

Hannah started shaking. "I-I...oh, shit! I don't know!"

"Indeed. It appears, in fact, that you don't know *anything.* Mercy?"

Mercy just started bawling.

"Oh, for goodness' sake, Mercy! You are the *definition* of the term 'Tits on a bull.'" Then the dagger-glare shot back to me.

Fuck, I thought. I think that a lot. "Nostalgia is important because it reminds us not only of where we came from, but it enforces who we really are. Driving these old roads, for example—like you said, Miss Kezzy. It's not so much the fact that we're driving on the road, it's that we're driving on a piece of our history."

Kezzy's face kind of went blank, and her mouth opened. "I myself could not have answered the question more perfectly. Your perseverance, Ann, as well as your intuition, attention to detail, and your ability to subjectify, is slowly but surely forging you into a penultimate Alpha House pledge, and you're certainly the cream of this crop. I'm very proud of you. And, now? For your diligence, you shall be rewarded." She handed me a pack of Krimpets.

My hands shook as I held the pack. "You're, you're *serious*, Miss Kezzy?"

"Why, of course, Ann. Perseverance bids reward."

I eyed the pack. "Let me guess, Zenas wiped his ass with these, didn't he? Or rubbed his dick on them..."

Kezzy laughed. "Oh, Ann! Don't be so cynical! Those Krimpets are unopened, untampered with, and untouched."

The back of the pack *was* sealed. I opened it, broke off one Krimpet, looked at it, sniffed it.

It smelled *wonderful*.

I turned it upside-down and took a bite. That perfect butterscotch icing *melted* on my tongue. I chewed ever-so-slowly. Then all that flavor burst into my mouth. My fingers tingled. My toes curled. It was *so good* I whined and my eyes rolled back in their sockets. I didn't woof it down, oh, no. Probably took me five minutes just to eat the first Krimpet.

It was the best thing in the world.

But the thing about Krimpets was, there were *three* per pack. I broke off the second one, was about to take the first bite, but then I looked at Hannah and Mercy.

They looked like two puppies staring back at me...

I paused.

"Really, Ann," Kezzy said. "You're actually thinking about giving the other two to your cohorts? You want to give them *your* reward, which *you alone* have earned, while Hannah and Mercy have earned nothing? Really?"

Their faces were so long, their eyes so big.

I wanted those other two Krimpets more than *anything*, but I just sputtered, "Oh, fuck it! Here!" and gave them each a Krimpet.

I swear they made noises like two pigs at feeding time. Hannah about *inhaled* hers, and Mercy looked like she was having the first orgasm of her life. And, get this. The two ungrateful bitches didn't even say thank you, but when they were done, I kind of — well, I just felt good about myself.

"You have yet to cease to impress me, Ann," Kezzy said. "It's very much an Alpha House signature, for one sister to share with her other sisters."

"But we're not sisters yet, Miss Kezzy," I pointed out. "We're only pledges, and we still have the rest of Pledge Week to get through, don't we?"

"Indeed, you do. And, girls, I might as well inform you that the day's trials are not quite over. We're not merely out on a nice leisurely drive through the countryside. Tonight, we have a more defined purpose. Because, you see, *tonight*" — she raised a finger. "*Tonight*...we're going Old-Manning..."

☠ ☠ ☠

OKAY. You're probably getting the idea. Old-Manning? *What the fuck is that?* I thought. I mean, it's pretty obvious, isn't it? But it didn't occur to me at all when she said it, because I didn't think that even Kezzy could be that twisted.

I was *way way* wrong.

Few minutes later, Zenas pulled the Rolls up in front of a little building back up in the hills. There were lights on and several beat-up, pieces-of-shit-looking cars there. The sign read

51

Going Monstering

AMERICAN LEGION - DUNWICH POST.

That's when it occurred to me. *Old Manning. You gotta be shitting me...*

"Isn't this a tavern for, like, old people?" Hannah asked when we all got out of the Rolls. Zenas stayed in the car, guess it wasn't cool for a dude in a maid suit to go into a public place. "Guys who were in the military," I said. "Old men. Get it? Old men? Old Manning?"

Kezzy walked behind us, smiling away.

"What did she mean by Old Manning?" Mercy asked.

"Oh, I don't know, Mercy, but let me take a wild guess and say that we're probably gonna have to blow some old men."

"Very perceptive, Ann," Kezzy said.

Mercy looked cross-eyed in fear. "What? *Blow?* You mean, like, like...we'll have to perform *oral sex* on them?"

Kezzy laughed. "You're finally starting to catch on."

I opened the rickety door, then we all walked in, but Mercy kept tugging on my sleeve. "Ann? Ann? She's joking, right? *Right?*"

"We're gonna have to suck off some old men, Mercy. So just deal with it," I told her, absolutely disgusted with the whole thing.

"Holy shit," Hannah whispered. "I don't know if I can do it."

"And I *can't* do it!" Mercy blurted. "It's a sex-act out of wedlock! It's a *sin!*"

"Mercy, you need to get off that sin kick if you want to even stand a *chance* of passing your initiations."

"Sound advice," Kezzy said.

It was a typical ramshackle old place with wooden walls and a wooden floor, some shitty tables and chairs, plus a long bar full of glowing BUD LIGHT signs and shit like that. The bartender had a cowboy hat on, and a white handle-bar mustache. He looked about seventy but the other two old coots sitting at the bar *had* to be in their eighties. One was fat with giant

52

moles all over his face and a hat that said I WAS ON OMAHA BEACH. Shit, I didn't know there were beaches in Nebraska. The other old fuck had a Navy hat on and looked like a fuckin' skeleton covered with saggy white skin.

"Howdy, gals," the bartender said, then he tipped his hat to Kezzy. "Weer always happy to have Alpha House folks in our bar."

Kezzy introduced us. The bartender was Henry, Mole Face was Albert, and the grinning skeleton was Nahum or some fucked up name like that. They all wore blue jeans and suspenders. Nahum took one look at Mercy, whistled through his dentures, and rubbed his crotch. "I'se the oldest heer so's I get fust dibs. I'll take that skinny 'un thar."

But the other two guys, Mole Face and the bartender, were kind of arguing. "I'm the *customer*, Henry! Jesus H. Christ! I was fightin' the Waffen SS on D-Day when I weern't but seventeen!"

"Ee-yuh? An' I fought the blammed Chinese'n North Koreans, so's yew kin kiss my ass!"

"Aw, Korean weren't a real war, it was a no-dick war!"

"Gentlemen, gentlemen!" Kezzy interrupted. "There's only one fair way to settle such disputes." She took out a coin and flipped it.

"Tails!" the bartender yelled.

"Tails, you win, Henry!" Kezzy announced.

Mole Face frowned.

"Miss Kezzy?" I asked. "What were you flipping the coin over?"

"Well, Ann, are you sure you want to know?"

"Yeah."

"The loser gets *you*."

I really appreciated that.

"But, but, Miss Kezzy?" Hannah asked. "These men are really *old*. Men this old can't get erections, can they?"

"Yeah," I whispered. "Ain't no way they'll get their dicks hard."

Going Monstering

"Oh, is that so, Ann?" Kezzy snipped at me. "Dr. Willet is eighty-six years old, yet he *got his dick hard*, did he not? Hard enough to stick up *your ass?*"

"Well, yeah, Miss Kezzy, but—"

"And you can thank pharmacological science for that," and then she pointed to the bar where the three old fucks were clinking their beer glasses together, then chuckling as they all popped blue, oval-shaped pills.

"Viagra!" Kezzy exclaimed.

"Great," I sputtered. "That's just fuckin' great..."

The bartender pulled his pants down and sat bare-assed on the bar. "Step right up heer, you big honey-pie," he said to Hannah, "and start talkin' tew the Captain." The guy was already half hard just looking at Hannah, but Hannah looked like she was about to croak. "Oh my God, oh my God, oh my God!" she shrieked.

"Just do it, Hannah," I said. "Get it over with," and then I turned to Mole Face and sighed. The fat fuck was sitting on his barstool with his dick out. That ancient dick was bad enough but his moles grossed me out even more. They looked like a bunch of Sugar Babies sticking out of his face.

"No offense, fat-stuff," he said, "I mean abaout the coin toss. I like a woman with some meat on her bones but, shee-it, not *thet* much meat."

"Thanks a lot," I said.

He flapped his dick a couple times and it started to get hard but then I thought—*holy motherfucking SHIT*—'cos that's when I saw the he had moles on his cock too.

But Mercy screamed.

The skeleton—Nahum—was sitting in a chair, kind of clucking like a rooster, and he'd taken his pants all the way off. His fuckin' legs were like white broomsticks, I kid you not. It was easy to see what Mercy was screaming about. This guy, he was pulling a full boner that was almost as big as Zenas's, and his bag was sagging halfway to the floor with nuts in it like a couple

54

of baby fists. Just seeing this corpse-skinny old withered skull-faced cretin with that big hard-on sticking up was *terrifying*.

"Mercy, you've never blown a guy before, have you?"

"No!" she shrieked.

"Well, first of all, you don't *blow* into it—and don't ask me why they call it a 'blowjob' 'cos I don't know. You just kind of get your mouth spitty inside, then slide it over his pecker and move your lips up and down over it, and you suck while you're doing it. It's easy."

"No, it's not!" God, she had an annoying shriek. "It's a sin!"

Here we go with that again. "It's not a sin, Mercy, and here's why. Because you're not doing it as an act of lust. *Lust* is the sin, right?"

"Well...yeah."

"You're doing it so you can get into the sorority, and if you get into the sorority, then you will improve as a person. And if you improve as a person, then you improve as a *Christian.* Right?"

It was just some B.S. right off the top of my head, but she kind of fidgeted, and peeped, "Well, I never thought of it that way before."

"So just do it. We're all going to do it. It's for a greater good."

"Well said, Ann," Kezzy approved.

"Come on, Slim!" the skeleton cackled. "Quit'cher girlie-talk and get tew suckin' on this heer meat-pole!"

I patted her on the shoulder. Then she walked over, got down on her knees, and got to it.

Hannah was already going a mile a minute, and her guy was making noises like a cowboy at a rodeo. Mole Face grinned and flexed his boner for me. Fuck. I just leaned over and started sucking.

It was awful, pathetic, and ridiculous: three 19-year-old girls blowing *really old men*. Of course, my guy's crotch stunk, but by then I was cauterized to it. After the tongue baths? Shit. "Durn, fat-stuff, what yew en't got in looks yew shuhly make up fer in dick-suckin'." With every stroke my lips bumped over the moles, and when his balls started to bunch up, the moles on his sack stuck out more, like big ticks.

"Ee-yuh, ee-yuh, ee-yuh," the skeleton was grunting.

The bartender was hooting "Suck thet dick, *suck* it!"

My guy was holding my head. "This heer fat 'un's one *hail* of a fuck-face! Go, fat-stuff! Go!"

Five minutes went by, then ten.

Then fifteen.

These old fucks may have had full boners but they sure as shit weren't getting off. Five more minutes after *that*, my fuckin' *mouth* was starting to hurt.

Finally, the bartender banged both fists on the bar and cracked, "*Theeeeer's* the dick-snot, honey! *Theeeeeeeer* it is!" and then Hannah lifted her head off his crotch, stood in shock a moment, and gulped it down.

"Git it, fat-stuff!" Mole Face was huffing, and I was pretty close to snapping from that "fat-stuff" crack. You can only shit on fat people so long before they just say to hell with it.

"You should consider yourself honored," Kezzy said behind me. "Albert is a combat veteran of the European Theater. He fought the Germans during the Allied invasion."

I didn't know *shit* about the Civil War, but all I could think was, *Well, then it's too bad the fuckin' Germans didn't KILL the asshole, because if he says "fat-stuff" one more time, I just might pop his old balls and bite his cock clean off.*

Eventually he came too, "oozing" more than "shooting." I guess whatever kind of sperm-pump a guy's got must wear out when they get this old. *One, two, three,* I thought, then grimaced, then let it slide down my throat.

"Suck and swallow, girls, suck and swallow," Kezzy was saying. "That's the Alpha House Pledge Credo. Remember, there's no *spitting* in Alpha House. Ladies don't spit. They swallow."

Terrific.

But ten minutes later, Mercy still hadn't gotten the skeleton off. Her head wagged up and down, black hair flapping like bat wings. Eventually, she stopped, looked up in a horrified daze, and wailed, "It's not happening! He's never gonna, gonna—"

"Shoot his load?" Kezzy said with a giant smile. "Get his nut?"

"Wal, now, Slim, yew young 'uns gots ta have patience. Juss yew git back ta suckin' an' I'll kick out the snot in no time. 'Nother ten, twenny minutes, I 'spose. No big deal."

It *was* a big deal. "Fuck that shit," I said. "We're not waiting that long—Mercy, spit on your finger and stick it up his ass while you're sucking."

Her eyes almost popped out. "I'm not doing that! It's, it's dirty. My finger'll have his *poop* on it!"

"For shit's sake!" I stomped over, spat on her finger and—

"Ooo, ee-yuh. Thet theer's the ticket," the old crank chuckled.

—slipped it up his ass.

"*Very* resourceful, Ann," Kezzy complimented.

Mercy about screamed but I was so sick of this shit that I grabbed her head and pushed her mouth back down of the codger's hard-on. Then I started pumping her head like it was a bicycle pump. "Now, *suck*, Mercy! And wiggle your finger around! Shit, we'll be older than he is by the time you're done fooling around!"

Mercy was gagging, but I didn't care. She had to learn, and *I* was gonna help her. In another minute, the old stick started squirming, his lips stuck out like fish lips, and he goes, "Aw, eeeeeeeee-YUH! Heer she goes!"

Mercy looked like someone put a pitchfork in her back when the guy came in her mouth. She actually slammed back on the floor, popping her brown finger out, and when she started crying, the old fucker's load spilled out of her mouth.

Kezzy crossed her arms, doing that foot-tapping thing of hers. "I see that Mercy doesn't remember her Pledge Credo,

57

hmm? Suck and swallow?"

"*Huh?*"

"You let the guy's nut fall out of your mouth!" I bellowed. "You're supposed to swallow!"

Kezzy nodded. "And I can only think of one way to rectify the matter."

"You're gonna have to eat his cum off the floor, Mercy," I told her. "Otherwise, she'll kick you out."

Mercy looked delirious, which I think was pretty understandable. "Huh? *Eat?*"

I grabbed her head, pushed her face to the floor. "Just do it, Mercy! Then it'll all be over and we can go!"

I guess it was pretty cruel of me to force her to eat this old asshole's load off the floor, but the only reason I was doing it was to keep her in the sorority. And I gotta hand it to the guy — for someone older than Moses — he popped out a *lot* of cum.

Mercy gagged. Mercy convulsed. She got up two licks, but then that was it for her. She flopped over and passed out.

Kezzy looked down at the remaining splats of sperm. She shook her head. "That's a shame. I was actually rooting for her."

"Oh, come on, Miss Kezzy! Don't kick her out just 'cos of that," I begged the bitch. "She got some of it up."

"*Some*, I'm afraid, isn't enough. Mercy has failed this phase of her hazing. She's out."

"But she *tried!*" I yelled. "It's not her fault she got so grossed out she lost fuckin' consciousness!" An idea flashed. "Wait! Miss Kezzy, please. If I lick up the rest, will you let her stay?"

Tap-tap-tap-tap. "Yet another demonstration of your character, Ann. *That's* what Alpha House is all about. Very well. Your sacrifice is her gain."

"Wow, Ann!" Hannah exclaimed. "You're hardcore!"

Yeah, I guess I fuckin' am, I thought and then clunked down and licked that ancient shit-head's jizz right off the dirty floor. It's bad enough getting it straight from the tap, but this way? Fuck. It's like licking it up after a redneck hocks a loogie on the floor, only *this* loogie happened to come out of his dick. *That's* what I kept thinking while I was doing it.

Charming.

"Holy jumpin' horse feathers!" Henry the barkeep said when I was done. He was leaning over the skeleton and had a finger to his neck.

"Say it en't so!" cried Mole Face.

"Nahum's shuh as hail up'n had a heart attack! He's dead!" He pronounced "heart" as *hot*, and "dead" as dee-ed.

One good look at the guy said it all. He was out for eternity and already turning whiter than he normally was. Big smile on his face, though.

"Thet skinny gal done sucked ole Nahum to death!"

"Wal, he *did* have hisself a bad ticker."

"Oh my God, oh my God!" Hannah shrieked. "It's murder!"

I smirked. "Don't be a dope, Hannah. It's his own fault, willful negligence or death by misadventure or some shit."

"Sounds like perhaps a *pre-law* curriculum might be in order for you," Kezzy said, laughing.

"Yeah, a pretty good rule of thumb is *don't* put your dick in a 19-year-old's mouth when you've got a heart condition and are pushing *fuckin' ninety*." I sneered at the old fuck. "*Fuck* him. Looks to me like he's been alive ten years too long anyway. No fuckin' *wonder* Social Security is running out of money — too many withered old *fucks* like him still walking the earth."

Kezzy's mouth fell open. "Ann, your cynicism knows no bounds. You're *completely bereft* of compassion for the elderly."

"*Fuck* the elderly, and fuck *him*. We did the job, so let's get out of here."

Me and Hannah dragged Mercy out to the Rolls and stuffed her in back. Zenas was chuckling. "Damn, what a day," I mumbled.

"I'se *bet* it was!" Zenas honked.

"I think that guy in the cowboy hat was deliberately trying to rupture my tonsils," Hannah said. She made a smacking sound. "And —*jeez!*— I hate the taste of sperm!"

"I gotta a feeling we need to stock up on a *lot* of Listerine this week," I said.

Kezzy got back in. "I'm very proud of you girls, you especially, Ann. Going the extra mile will always serve you in life."

Zenas started the car and began to pull out, but then I jumped up. "Zenas! Hold up a sec! There's something I *gotta* do!" and then I got out and jogged across the lot. See, one of the old beat-to-shit cars there had a bumper sticker that read I WAS ON OMAHA BEACH. I got in, pulled my pants down, and took a nice yogurty shit in the front seat, then I wrote a note in the cigarette film on the windshield, COMPLIMENTS OF FAT-STUFF.

After that, I felt *much* better.

When Mercy woke up, we didn't tell her that her blowjob had fuckin' *killed* the skeleton-looking guy. She was enough of a head-case. "I can't believe I passed!" she said.

"You can thank Ann for that," Kezzy said, and then she explained how I'd done the clean-up job.

Mercy started crying. "Oh, Ann! You're my *best* friend!" and she wrapped her arms around me and gave me a hug. "How can I ever thank you?"

I had to wrench her left hand *away* from me. "You can thank me by keeping that hand *away* from me!"

"Yeah," Hannah said with a grimace and fanned her face. "P-U! Your finger *stinks!*"

"I *thought* I smelt a asshole finger somewheer," Zenas said.

Asshole finger —Jesus. That's the course my life was taking. I guess it took Mercy a minute to remember. She sniffed her finger...

And screamed.

We made Mercy keep her hand out the window during the drive home.

Kezzy turned around a sec while she was fussing with her perfect fuckin' blond hair and said, "You're finished for the night, girls, and I'm delighted that you all passed your second day of initiation." She batted her lashes. "That's the *good* news."

Me, Hannah, and Mercy all looked scared shitless at each other.

"Uh, Miss Kezzy?" I asked. "What's...the *bad* news?"

Now the bitch was plucking her eyebrows in the visor mirror. "The bad news is that tomorrow will be *exponentially* worse."

T**HE** nights after each hazing were pretty much the same, the nightmares, I mean. First I'd dream that Joseph Corwan, from the portrait downstairs, would come into my room and fuck with me one way or another. He'd jerk off, rub his dick in my face, feel me up, put his face between my legs, whatever. I could see it but I could never *feel* it. Then he'd disappear like a ghost and a little later, Zenas would lope in and spit on me, blow his nose in my mouth, or hock a big ole loogie on my twat—gross shit like that, and sometimes he'd jerk off afterwards and make me eat his nut. Then a little later, Kezzy would be sitting on my face and just when I kind of started to like it, the snake would drop out of her cooze and slide down my throat.

And sometime later?

I'd either wake up, or *dream* I'd woken up, and I'd be lying there paralyzed, and I'd hear that weird shit at a really low volume, over and over for what felt like hours, those words in Kezzy's voice but words that made no sense: *Shub neb hyr'ik eb hyr'k. Ogthrod ai'f geb'l, ee'h yog-sothoth...*

I mean, my memory's for shit. I never remembered anything; Christ, I couldn't recite the Star Spangled Anthem to save my life. But every morning, I could remember those words, that

Going Monstering

gobbledegook, Shub neb hyr'ik eb hyr'k. Ogthrod ai'f geb'l, ee'h yog-sothoth...

Fuckin' weird.

But we all felt really great when we got home that second night after the cluster-fuck at the American Legion. Kezzy let us eat some yogurt, then we all went up and took a shower. The shower was like a mini locker room shower, four nozzles, and after having to give each other a tongue-bath, none of us were self-conscious about being nude in front of anyone else.

"What do you suppose we'll have to do tomorrow?" Hannah asked, sudsing up.

"Something really fucked up," I suggested. "Best not to think about it."

Mercy's face looked maniacal while she scrubbed her finger. "One thing I'm *not* doing is sticking my finger up any more stinky *butts!*"

"Don't be too sure," I said, cranking my water up hot. I opened my mouth under the spray hoping to wash out the taste. "She warned us the worst is yet to come, that prissy hosebag. God knows what her demented brain will think of — something really worthy of the sewer."

"Oh, NO!" Mercy wailed. She held her finger up. "I've got that old man's poop under my fingernail!"

For fuck's sake. "You're lucky that cocksure blond cunt didn't make you fist the guy."

"*Huh?*" Mercy said, eyes bugging. "*Fist?* What's — "

"Don't ask." She was about as naive as they got. I'm glad I was able to help her get through the shit today, but I wondered how well she'd hold up during the rest of the week. I had to frown at her, though. I mean, she really did have a *lot* of pubic hair, and when it was wet it hung down like a soggy black mop. "And, Mercy, take some advice from a friend and trim your bush, huh? That's a *shitload* of hair you got down there."

She looked baffled. "But...it's my natural state! It's the way God wants me!"

"I seriously doubt that God cares how you keep your bush, Mercy." I guess I was being hypocritical 'cos I know my box looked like shit, just like the rest of me. But at least I kept mine trimmed. "I mean, how much do you weigh?"

"Well, a hundred," she said.

The bitch. "Then I guarantee only ninety of that is you and the other ten is pubic hair."

"Yeah," Hannah said. "Do yourself a favor and trim it. These days guys don't like a girl who's real hairy down there."

Mercy shrugged. "I don't care what *guys* like. I guess when I get married some day and my husband wants me to, I will. But since I'll never have sex out of wedlock, I'm not really worrying about it."

"En't no call ta shave that theer girlie hair," that awful New England drawl echoed in the shower.

"What are you doing here?" I yelled at Zenas. "And—" My jaw nearly disconnected from my head when I got a load of what he was wearing. The other girls were actually shrieking.

Zenas was wearing a fuckin' *bikini*. No bull. The hairy, muscular chest was gross enough, and so was the top, which had sponge balls or something in the cups. But the *grossest* part was the bottoms. See, the crotch had a slit in it, and from there all his junk hung out.

"Oh, man!" I bellowed. "You look ridiculous in that! Get the fuck out!"

"Yeah!" Hannah shouted. "Pledge Week or not, *men* aren't allowed in the girls' shower!"

"They is if'n Kezzy says so," he replied.

"What?"

Zenas nodded, while kind of flexing all those muscles. "Ee-yuh, it was Kezzy who told me to come up heer." He started fondling his limp meat. "Fer yew're punishment, fattie."

"Punishment?"

The next voice to echo through the shower was Kezzy's.

Correction: *fuckin'* Kezzy's.

Going Monstering

"It's bewildering, Ann, that you can do so well one minute, then completely *fuck up* the next," her bodiless voice drifted. It was from a speaker hidden somewhere, which could only mean—

"You've got a microphone in the *shower?*"

"I believe I made it quite plain last night that Alpha House is rife with microphones. Really, Ann? 'Prissy hosebag?' 'Demented brain,' worthy of the 'sewer?' Oh, and my favorite thus far. 'Cocksure blond *cunt.*'"

I might as well have shoved my own foot in my mouth. I fell to my knees looking up at wherever this hidden speaker was, and begged, "I'm sorry, Miss Kezzy! Please believe me!"

"Oh, I do indeed believe you're sorry, Ann. And you'll be even sorrier once your punishment has been dispensed." She chuckled. "Let's just hope that a certain other part of your body is as large as your mouth..."

Hannah and Mercy were hugging each other, and screaming like a couple five-year-olds on a really scary roller coaster when Zenas got down on his knees behind me and started sudsing up my crack with the soap, but they screamed *twice* as loud when he'd stroked himself fully hard and, without even a pause, pushed it all in my ass to the balls. I'm not much of a screamer, but even *I* screamed at that.

"Nooooo!" Mercy shrieked.

"It's way too big for that!" Hannah yelled.

"Aw, new. Gals' assholes're like wild bucks. All yew gotta dew is bust 'em in."

I swear, it was like having a fuckin' eggplant shoved up there, the fat-end first. That's how much it hurt. I breathed like someone about to drown while that monster was plunging in and out. Zenas chuckled kind of to the rhythm and reached under to slap my belly fat while he was doing it. "Ee-yuh, juss like a big piglet, yew is, heh, heh, heh."

"Oh, come on, man!" I begged, and now I was crying like Mercy always did.

Edward Lee

"Ooo, whut's thet I feel up'n thar? Yer gall bladder, mebbe? Let's juss see if we curn't pop it..."

"Stop it!" someone else bellowed, and the surprising thing was...it was Mercy. She'd broken away from Hannah to boldly come forward—mousy hair sopping wet, gritting her teeth, *rage* in her eyes. "Enough is enough, Zenas! You can't just *sodomize* girls any time you want! So STOP DOING THAT!"

It had to be the first time in Mercy's whole fuckin' life that she actually got mad and yelled at someone. But once she did, Zenas stopped sod-pounding my butt, and he just looked up at her.

"So's...yew want me ta *stop?*"

"Yes! Stop it!"

"Wal, awright, but theer's one condition. See, if'n I pull my cock aout'a fattie's backside, then I'll be slidin' right into yours, stringbean."

"Keep doing it, Zenas! Don't stop!" Mercy started yelling. "It's no big deal! She's done it a bunch of times before any way!"

"Thought so," he chuckled, then got back to pounding.

"Oh, thanks a lot, Mercy!" I yelled. How do you like people, huh? You help them out but do they ever return the favor? Fuck no. Couple minutes later, by the time I felt like I'd had my ass-hole sewer-rooted, Zenas got his nut. He must've thought my ass was a crankcase and figured I was a quart low 'cos that's how much it felt like he pumped in there. Then he pulled out, sudsed up his junk, and was kind enough to rub it all around in my hair before he rinsed off.

"Theer. Mebbe *thet*'ll tone down some'a yer sass. And if'n it durn't, I guess I'll juss have ta bring a buddy ovuh heer, an' we'll git *both* our cocks up yer ass at the same time."

"Don't bother!" I yelled. "I'm now 100-percent sass-free!"

"Juss make shuh yew stay thet way."

Zenas loped off, and that's when I called it a night.

My ass hurt so bad the next morning, it felt like I'd just had fuckin' colon surgery. Right off the bat, Kezzy asked, "Why,

65

Going Monstering

Ann...are you unwell? You appear to be in pain with every step you take."

"That's because I got a dick the size of a Pringles can rammed up my ass last night...Miss Kezzy," I said.

"Yes, and you're aware as to *why*, aren't you?"

"Punishment," I kind of peeped. "For running my mouth..."

"Good. I hope you learned a lesson."

You *bet* I did.

We had more salt-free pretzel rods while she and Zenas scarfed down these giant crab-meat omelets. I'll bet that bitch could out-eat that Japanese guy who'd won the world hot-dog-eating contest. But, you know, that's another thing you constantly notice when you're fat. The slim, beautiful people can stuff their faces all they want and never gain an ounce, but me? If I eat, like, *one* candy bar, I put on five fuckin' pounds before I'm even done eating the motherfucker.

Anyway, here's how the deal went for the next four days. Twice a day we'd go "something-ing." The Old Manning on that second night was nothing compared to what Kezzy had in store for us, and she wasn't kidding when she said the rest would be "exponentially worse" than blowing those old turds at the American Legion. First up? Are you ready for this?

"This afternoon, ladies," Kezzy announced after her crab-meat omelet, and then she paused and grinned at us all. "We're going Kenneling."

I ain't kiddin' ya. Kenneling. She piled us into the Rolls and Zenas took us straight to the Happy Doggie Pet Motel, and there were definitely some happy doggies *at* this place. That psycho Kezzy paid off the kennel staff to give us the green light—they had three dogs waiting for us: Hannah got the German Shepherd, Mercy got the Jack Russell, and me?

I got the Great Dane.

Mercy and Hannah kind of went into shock just looking at these dogs, but I set an example, I guess. *It's a state of mind*, I told myself. I just had to get into that state, and then I could do anything.

No way in a million years would I have even *thought* about doing something like this a week ago. But now? The carrot Kezzy was dangling in front of me was my fuckin' inheritance.

I was *not* going to throw in the towel now.

Hannah and Mercy started screaming when I got down on my knees and just started...*doing* it to the Great Dane. His name was George, by the way, and he was a big ass dog. You ever seen the *dick* on a 150-pound dog? It's like a sheath, and inside the sheath is this long pink flesh-covered bone. You start sucking on the end of that sheath, then the pink part starts to come out. George's tail-nub was wagging away while I had my face down there. I just kept my mind blank...and I did it. (Oh, and the fuckin' thing's balls had to be *twice* the size of a dude's.) It was the grossest thing I'd ever done in my life, but I'll tell you, once I got started, it kind of broke the ice, then Hannah and Mercy started doing it too—all the while Kezzy stood back with her arms crossed right next to the seriously fucked-up-in-the-head kennel workers and they were laughing so hard they were making every other dog in the kennel bark. I was really surprised that Mercy did it but then, she had it easier 'cos the Jack Russell was tiny compared to the mutts Hannah and I had to blow. Believe it or not, we all got our dogs off and we choked the doggie jizz down without a hitch. (I won't bother going into just how *much* a Great Dane comes, or what it tastes like.) Sure, it was the lowest point of my entire life but when I was done...

I felt that I'd really *accomplished* something, something that very few people would have the guts to do. It made me think of what Kezzy said that one time, about me having "resolve." Yeah, I fuckin' guess so. When you suck a dog's dick to get into a sorority, one thing you've definitely got is resolve.

Things got a little out of hand when George started trying to fuck Mercy, but I gotta tell ya, it *was* funny. She passed out just like at the American Legion, so me and Hannah dragged her out of that fuckin' zoo. You should've heard the dogs barking

Going Monstering

when we left.

Only in America, huh? Next time you check Fido into a pet motel, you might want to think twice 'cos you never know. Some whacked out sorority pledges might be blowing your pets while you're on vacation.

After the dogs, we figured nothing could be worse than that, but—

We were wrong.

See, that night, Kezzy took us "Bumming."

Little homeless shelter in Wilbraham. Took us a long time to get there. "I'm not doing it, I'm not doing it!" Mercy was having a conniption in the Rolls, and Hannah sat there the whole ride, crying with her face in her hands. "You're the team leader, Ann," Kezzy said. "So... Rally your team." I guess she was right in a way. I shook both the girls around and said, "Listen! We can't quit now! Are we quitters? Were we quitters at the American Legion last night? Were we quitters at the dog motel? *Fuck* no! We're Alpha House girls, and we *don't quit!* We've come this far, and we're gonna keep going! It's easy. We got through the dogs, didn't we? We'll just keep our minds blank and do it, and before we know it, it'll be over and we'll be another day closer to getting into the sorority! Just follow my lead!"

I guess that roused them a little, but when we finally got to this stinky place, I had a real low feeling in my gut. Kezzy paid off the two social workers there, and they took us to a room full of bunk beds, and this room had, like, ten bums in it. Fuckin' guys with mops of gray hair, rotten clothes, rotten sneakers, all sitting around eating canned sardines and chuckling with black teeth. Kezzy announced, "Several days ago, girls, you proved what you were made of by licking others privates after having not washed in a day. But *these* gentlemen?" She extended her hand. "They haven't washed in *months.*"

Hannah and Mercy moaned, so I just kept on being the team captain. "Who's first?" I asked, then just picked one sitting on his bunk picking his nose. He looked like fucking Santa Claus from hell with this big dirty beard full of lice and bits of food. "Drop

68

your pants, Pops. Let's get this party started." The guy pulled his pants down, then *peeled* down his underwear. I looked at the other girls. "Just hold your nose, keep your mind blank, and do it!" I yelled, and then I got on my knees and started sucking this homeless rummy's unwashed-for-months dick.

You should've heard these useless fucks all laughing while we were doing it. Lot of 'em had fleas, and I swear one guy had *ants* living in his crotch-hair. Then there was another guy with some rash all over half his head, and it looked like he had *shit* packed in his belly-button.

"Let's not forget the Alpha Pledge Credo, girls," Kezzy reminded. "Suck and swallow."

And that's what we did, all right. The worst smells I've ever known in my life were *those* smells. These guys all had old shit-smears in their shorts, horrendous smegma, and breath that could send Godzilla packing. And their jizz? It tasted even worse than the dog's. We each blew three guys but then there was that *tenth* one—the rash guy—so when we flipped a coin?

You *know* who lost.

The fuckin' guy's cock was, like, *slimy* with bum sweat, and there was, like, some kind of *grit* on it, too, and to tell you the truth, I almost couldn't get through it with him, but I knew damn well Hannah or Mercy wouldn't help me out. Then he kind of wet-farted while I was doing it, and it's a good thing I didn't have a gun on me, 'cos I would've capped that homeless waste product without thinking twice. Sent the stinky fuck to that great shelter in the sky. I'd always felt sorry for homeless people, but now? Fuck 'em. Wouldn't bother me if the state just ground 'em up for fertilizer or something, make prisoner food out of them. Chain 'em to stationary bicycles connected to generators for electricity—hey, there's an idea!

I could see little bugs *moving around* on this loser's balls, and when he came, it was like... Well, he must've had something wrong with him 'cos it tasted like he had blood in his jizz.

But it all went down the hatch anyway.

Going Monstering

When we got back in the car, all nauseous and dizzy, it really was a confidence-booster to hear Kezzy say, "Congratulations, ladies. Only two more days of hazing to go. I couldn't be more proud."

I believed it.

"This all went very well," she was saying. "It's the first time we've had a Bumming session. Last few years the pledges would go Nursing Homing, but that was just too grim. And — you'll be pleased to hear *this* — when I was a pledge the S.S.S. made us go Retarded Peopling, and *that* just got way out of hand. In the old days, the girls would have to go Chain-ganging, and I can only imagine what a hoot that was. Can't do it anymore, though, because prison chain-gangs violate the Constitutional rights of the prisoners. We can't have *that* now, can we?"

"*Fuck* them," I said.

"Oh, and another favorite of the old days was Horsing, but that stopped after several girls got killed. Hooves to the head, things like that."

I guess that was the Alpha House history lesson, but we were so brain-cooked after blowing those bums we barely heard her.

Big stomach-aches kicked our asses that night. And Mercy wasn't the same anymore. She didn't talk like she usually did, and she just kind of walked around with her eyes really wide, whispering prayers to herself. We scrubbed the living shit out of ours mouths, took an hour-long steam shower, then threw out the clothes we'd worn that day. Bum-stink haunted me for a long time.

I woke up in the middle of the night, after more of those fucked up nightmares and then dreaming those weird words in Kezzy's voice.

I looked under my bunk and saw Hannah quivering under her sheets, and I could only hope her nightmares weren't as bad as mine. But then I looked across to the other bunk, and there was Mercy sitting on the edge of her mattress staring into the dark.

"Mercy. Are you all right?"

"I'm inundated in sin," she whispered, a hand to her heart.

"Bullshit. It's just hazing. Every frat house and sorority has it."

"No," she moaned. "My sins are unabsolvable. I've affronted God, I'll incur His wrath. I'll *never* be forgiven."

More holy roller stuff. "Sure you will," I tried to console her. "This is just a circumstance where we gotta do gross stuff we'd *never* do any other time. If we get into the sorority, we'll do better in college, we'll graduate and make something of ourselves. All this hazing stuff is just making a sacrifice for something more important, right?"

Her giant eyes looked up at me in the dark.

"Look, doesn't it say in the Bible that you should obey your oppressors because the spirit of God can *never* be oppressed?"

"Yes...it does."

It was just more jive I made up, but this time I don't guess it was working. Mercy was fried crispy—I could tell by her eyes. She reached under her pillow, put her Ozzy Osborne cross on, and went back to sleep.

Either the bums or the dogs had broken her. *She'll be all right in the morning,* I told myself.

I got up. No way I could sleep. I walked down the dark hall in my oversized nightgown, listening. No sound at all. The door to the library was still locked—for some reason, I was dying to see that book Kezzy was reading in the gazebo the other night—and when I peeked into Kezzy's room, her bed was empty. Downstairs, the grandfather clock said it was past 3 a.m.

What was I doing? What would I tell Kezzy if she caught me wandering around, or what if *Zenas* did? The motherfucker would probably butt-fuck me again with that *hog* he had for a cock. I caught myself staring at the old painting—Joseph Corwan. I wondered what the old guy would think if he knew what kind of crazy-psycho shit was going on at his college...

Next thing I knew, I was looking out the kitchen window.

Going Monstering

There she is again! Kezzy was at the gazebo, a candle burning on the table. She was standing there buck-naked with her perfect 10 body, reading from that book again. But this time...

Zenas was with her.

He was naked too and, now, seeing him *without* that dumbass maid's suit, the guy really was a stud and a half. But what were they doing? For a minute, they both turned their backs to the door.

I slipped outside and crept around the hedges.

Kezzy was whispering something that I couldn't quite hear, and then Zenas...

He started to kind of wobble in place like he was drunk, his head rolling around. I thought he was gonna fall down, but then he snapped out of it and came over to Kezzy.

She got down on her knees and began to blow him.

THIS *I've got to see*, I thought, so I crept closer, quiet as I could. I managed to get maybe four or five feet away behind those hedges, and I had a perfect view of Kezzy chugging away on Zenas's cock.

Damn, she looks like she needs a shoe horn, I thought. Zenas was so big, it stretched Kezzy's mouth out. She was getting all flushed and misty with sweat, and then she pulled her lips off and pulled both of his balls into her mouth. She started sucking on them like a couple of Tootsie Pops, while Zenas was slowly stroking his hard-on. Then he said the weirdest thing.

"What delights, my sweet. You are a profound fellatrice."

What the fuck? It didn't sound *anything* like Zenas's voice.

"And this vessel you've provided is particularly pleasing, my precious whore. So virile. I feel filled to the very *brim* with seed..."

What was this weird fuckin' talk? They must be doing some silly play-acting thing 'cos there was no trace of Zenas's New England Redneck accent. If anything, he sounded like someone from olden times.

"And now, my sullied one, I have an unquenchable need to

sink deep into the purse of your womanhood..."

Practically panting, Kezzy tongued his balls out of her mouth and got up on the table right next to the big book. She had her ass on the edge and pulled her knees back. Then she almost whinnied like a horse when Zenas pushed his hard-on all the way in her.

He gave her a good throttling, banging the bitch's cooze so hard the fuckin' table was inching across the patio. Sounded like she came two or three times...

"And I see there's mischief afoot tonight. We've an inter-loper."

That's when both of them looked over right where I was hiding. They could see my *face* in the gap.

"Come out from there, Ann," Kezzy said.

I could've croaked on the spot. Did they know I was there all along?

I came out with my head down, while Zenas slowed his strokes.

"Ann. Take off your nightgown," Kezzy said.

"Oh, come on, Miss Kezzy," I begged. "It's humiliating for a fat girl like me to be naked in front of someone with a beautiful body like you."

"Why, Ann, I'm touched. What a nice compliment." She glared. "Now take off your fucking nightgown or I'll have Ze-nas sit on your face and shit in your mouth."

That's what I liked about Kezzy. She was such a warm, thoughtful person. I took off my gown, smirking.

"My, what a portly trollop, and quite uncomely," Zenas said. "Has this one any accreditations of note?"

"Oh, yes," and then Kezzy curled her finger at me and I stepped right up to where Zenas was practically busting her open with his cock. She reached up, grabbed my hair, and held my face down on her belly just as Zenas picked his pace back up.

"Ann, you know you'll have to pay for your Nosy Parkering, hmm? Now, open your mouth."

I did, and squeezed my eyes shut. *How much cum is she gonna make me eat in one day?* I thought.

Zenas popped his cock out of her just at the right time and fired three big slops of sperm straight into my mouth. Kezzy pushed up on my chin and made me swallow but Zenas was *still* getting his nut. Now Kezzy grabbed my hair tighter and moved my face around in front of the spurts. "Good, good," she whispered. "Paint her face."

Zenas hosed me down but good. When he was done, I was wearing a *mask* of his load.

"A proper and fitting anointment," Zenas said.

"What's with your voice?" I half-yelled.

Kezzy kept my cheek against her belly and that fucker Zenas? He put his half-hard dick right back in Kezzy's twat and started banging her again.

"I have the impression, Ann, it's not mere nosiness that makes you do stupid things like this, but instead a *burning* curiosity," Kezzy said. "For what is curiosity but proof of the quest for knowledge?"

I wasn't much listening to her because I knew what was coming. Zenas may have been a strapping, big-dicked stud, but he was also pretty young, and young guys could get off a couple times in a row. The guy *oozed* testosterone and I knew damn well he was gonna put more of it on me real soon.

"But there is some knowledge—knowledge so great, Ann, and so forbidden—that one must *earn* the right to be in its midst."

Zenas pulled out again and—BAM!—put another six or seven big belts of jizz right in my face. I was *sopped*.

"A delectable release," Zenas said.

"Come on! What's with your voice?"

"The voice?" Kezzy cooed at me, and that bitch was *still* holding my head on her belly. "Your desire to know is so *keen*, so *blistering*."

"And what's that *book?*" I gasped.

She patted my head and just chuckled.

"Oh man, you're shitting me, right!" I yelled when I looked up and saw Zenas hard *again*. He was standing right there between Kezzy's legs beating off a mile a minute.

"Zenas is a very fertile young man, Ann," Kezzy said.

"Why don't you just give it a rest!" I yelled but when I did that Zenas grunted and plastered my face *again*. "Heer ya go," he chuckled in his regular redneck voice. "More'a my nut fer ya, lots more..."

If anything the asshole came *more* each time. Felt like ten spurts went right into my face. When he was finally done, he slapped his limp meat a couple times against my cheek. *Splat, splat, splat*. Nice touch. He really knew how to make a girl feel wanted. "I appreciate that, Zenas," I groaned. By now it felt like my whole head had been dunked in a bucket of cum. "Why do you sound like your old redneck self all of a sudden?"

"Let's just say," Kezzy answered, rubbing her fingers around in my cummy face, "that an aspect of Zenas had to *absquatulate*."

"*What?* What the fuck is that?"

"Nothing, dear. I'm just toying with you."

"Wal, thet's it fer me. Durn't think I cud get off another 'un... less'n yew want me ta try, Kezzy."

"No, no, no!" I bawled.

"Hmm, well, the prospect sounds interesting," Kezzy purred. "Go ahead, please, Zenas. Give it the All American College Try."

No bullshit. The guy stood there and started beating off *again!* Maybe thirty seconds later, he pulled another full boner. "For fuck's sake, man!" I yelled. "No guy can come four times in a couple minutes! It's impossible!"

"Oh, Ann," Kezzy said, "on wondrous nights such as these, *all* things are possible..."

The bitch wasn't kidding because a minute later, Zenas pumped out four or five more big splats of spunk. Christ, where did it all *come* from?

"Ee-yuh," he grunted. "Thet theer's what we call a serious cum-face," and then he laughed.

"You're quite the man for all occasions, Zenas," Kezzy told him. "Thank you."

"Yeah!" I yelled. "Thanks!"

He walked away into the backyard darkness; Kezzy let me up, and I felt all that spooge start to crawl down my face, then my neck, then my chest. "You may go now, Ann," Kezzy said. "No more Nosy Parkering for *you*, hmm?"

You got that right. Kezzy reached down to take the book but before she picked it up, I caught a split-second glimpse of it.

The two pages I could see were hand-written, big fancy cursive handwriting. The paper was yellowed it was so old. Along the top read:

Transcription into Phonetic English of Stanzas 115-130

What the hell did *that* mean?

"But before you go, Ann?" Kezzy grinned at me, her big bare breasts sticking out, all shiny with sweat. She glanced at the book, said, "Heb f'ulfh wm'gyr ee'a glubb—" and the next thing I knew I was lying in my bed, tired as shit but wincing from a killer headache. I felt a fast rocking motion, and that only made my head hurt more, but then I opened my eyes and saw Kezzy there. She was shaking me.

"Ann? Ann, wake up. I need to know what happened."

"Whuh..." I leaned up and squinted. "Kezzy?" and then the memory socked me right in the face. *The gazebo. Kezzy and Zenas. That book.*

"What happened?"

"You mean at the gazebo?" I said. "You tell me."

"Gazebo? I don't know what you mean. But why is Mercy

leaving?" she said and shook me again.

I looked across to Mercy's bunk. It was empty, and her suit-case was gone. "Leaving? I—"

"Ann, she's standing outside right now waiting for a cab. Did she snap?"

I got up. A *cab*? I was confused. All I could think about was the cum-bath at the gazebo. "She...sounded weird earlier. Her religion or something. She feels guilty about the stuff we had to do." Hannah was asleep in her bunk; she was actually sucking her thumb, and I think she whispered, "Mommy. She made me suck a dog's dick..." I went to the window and looked out. Sure enough, there was Mercy standing at the end of the driveway with her suitcase. I rushed outside.

A cab was pulling up just when I got to her. "Mercy, don't leave!"

"I have to, Ann. I'm inundated in sin." She dragged her suit-case to the cab. "You should leave too. This house is evil. *Kezzy* is evil."

"Oh, come on! It's just hazing, Mercy. I admit, it's a bit ex-treme, but...if you leave now you won't get into the sorority."

"And if I *don't* leave, I won't get into Heaven."

"But we're halfway done! You can hack it a little more," but I could tell by the long stare and the drone of her voice that she was cooked. Kezzy's gross-out three-ring circus had finished her.

"Come with me, Ann."

"No, I've come this far, I'm going to finish—"

She put her suitcase in the cab. "We can redeem ourselves together, at church."

"I'm really not into church, Mercy. I think you're overreact-ing."

Her big clunky cross glittered when she got in. "Goodbye, Ann. I'll pray for you," then she closed the door and the taxi drove off.

Kezzy stood at the front door in her skimpy Victoria's Secret nightie. "Well?"

"She's gone. She quit," I told her, kind of holding back how mad I was.

"That's so strange. She'd done so well thus far."

"She's a sheltered Christian virgin, Miss Kezzy," I all but yelled. "You can only make a person like that lick so many dirty butts and blow so many dogs, bums, and shitty old men before they just lose it. What did you think? She couldn't hack it."

Kezzy smirked. "It's all for the best in that case. We don't want girls who can't hack it."

"No, I guess you don't."

"Ann, really. You seem to be directing your angst at *me*. I didn't *make* her do anything, nor have I *made* you or Hannah do anything. You seem to think that this is just some grotesque game—"

"Well it is, isn't it? Making girls blow *dogs?*"

She rolled her eyes. "There you go again. You've made *your-selves* do it, simply by choosing to, and by choosing to, you demonstrate the necessary—"

"Yeah, yeah, I know. Fortitude. Resolve and all that."

"Um-hmm. Mercy couldn't hack it...but I very much hope that *you* can."

"Oh, I'll hack it, all right, Miss Kezzy," and I knew then, for sure, that I would. Just to spite her, I'd do everything she ordered, no matter how gross. I would *show* the bitch.

"And what was all that about at the gazebo tonight?"

She peered at me. "The gaz—"

"Come on, Miss Kezzy, you know what I'm talking about. You and Zenas, the candle, the book? The *jizz* party? The Let's See How Many Times We Can Get Zenas To Come In Ann's Face Party?"

She laughed but actually seemed surprised. "Ann, I haven't a clue what you're talking about."

"So you weren't at the gazebo earlier, with Zenas?"

"Of course not. I went to bed at nine o'clock," and then her eyes narrowed. "Ann. Are you taking drugs? Alpha House does *not* take druggies."

"I don't take drugs, jeez."

"Then it appears you've been having some *potent* sexual fantasies — dreams, Ann."

I stared at her. A dream? No, no, it couldn't have been, but when I brought my hands to my face, it was clean. There wasn't a *trace* of Zenas's load, and I couldn't smell it, either.

"Go to bed, Ann. You've had a trying day. Goodnight."

"G-goodnight, Miss Kezzy."

I watched her go back upstairs, her perfect little Barbie Doll body kind of sashaying in that skimpy nightie.

So — shit — I guess it really WAS a dream...

There'd been harder things to believe in my life, or maybe I just believed it because I *needed* to. The fucked up thing was, the next day? Me and Hannah were watching the news on TV after our pretzel-rod breakfast and that's when we learned that the night before, a taxi cab lost control on the main road, crashed, and burst into flames, killing the driver, a local man named William Hurley, as well as Dunwich Women's College freshman Mercy Dexter.

NEXT day was the fourth day. Kezzy put us in the car at about 10 and Zenas drove us out on more of those winding back roads. No one talked much about Mercy getting killed. All Kezzy said was "What a terrible accident," but you know, when she said that, she looked over at Zenas for a second and I swear the guy smiled. Or, well, maybe he really *didn't* smile, maybe I just thought he did 'cos I was getting paranoid. When you swallow as much cum as I did over those few

Going Monstering

days, *anyone* would be paranoid. Plus, I was still a little bugged about the whole "dream" thing the night before in the backyard. Shit.

Anyway, you're probably wondering. What did Kezzy have up her sleeve for us today? Let's see, we'd already been Old Manning, Kenneling, and Bumming. What was next?

"Today, ladies," Kezzy said, fussing with her lipstick in the visor mirror, "we're going Rednecking..."

Great. She was gonna make us blow a couple of rednecks, but when Zenas pulled the Rolls up at that dingy tavern I got the message fast that it would probably be more than a "couple."

The dive was called KRAZY WHIPPLE'S TAVERN. It wasn't even fuckin' 11 in the morning and the parking lot was *full* of redneck pickup trucks. I really *hate* rednecks, by the way. "The happy-hour crowd," Kezzy said. "Perfect."

When me, Hannah, and Kezzy walked in, I thought *Holy motherfucking SHIT*. The place was packed with the mangiest rednecks I've ever seen. I mean, these guys made the big dude in *Deliverance* look like Liberace. When we walked in, the place got quiet; everyone turned to look at us. Then someone cracked, "Hot damn! Looks like it's Pledge Week at Alpha House!" and then the joint broke into an uproar.

Hannah just stared at them all, but I grabbed Kezzy's arm. "Miss Kezzy? It looks like there's fifty or sixty dudes in this place. How many do we have to blow?"

"Why, *all* of them, Ann..."

The place knew the drill. A couple of rednecks pulled two chairs against the wall, then, "Clothes off, girls."

Awwwww, fuck, I thought.

"In front of *everybody*?" Hannah whined.

We heard a lot of "fattie" jokes, and a couple of those yokels were making moo-cow noises while looking right at me.

"Line up, guys, juss like last yeer!" one redneck blared, and then every fuckin' guy in the bar broke off and formed two lines, one at each chair.

It was bad enough standing there naked with everybody laughing at us and pointing, but it was even worse when Kezzy said, "Have a seat, ladies. And...*what's* the Alpha House Pledge Credo?"

"Suck and swallow," I croaked, then I looked at Hannah. "Come on. Let's get started. This might take a while."

Hannah hadn't even sat all the way down before some rube with Elvis hair had his dick in her mouth. But when I sat down—

CRACK!

—the chair broke.

See what I mean about my Karma? When *that* happened, the place was *roaring* laughter. Some of these guys were crying they were laughing so hard. Then some other 'neck slid *over* a bigger chair, sat me down in it, and stuck his dick right in my mouth. And just my luck—the guy had a foreskin full of dick-cheese, but I just thought, *Fuck it*, and started sucking.

It was madness. It was pandemonium. The uproar was so loud I couldn't hear myself think—sounded like the fuckin' Super Bowl. After sucking off four or five guys, I looked around and saw that my line was longer than Hannah's. Figures. *Suck and swallow, suck and swallow*, I kept repeating to myself, and one after another, the hard dicks stepped up and sunk in my chops. Lot of them stunk—of course!—and some had day-old pussy-stink on them, or dried cum-tracks in their pubic hair. One guy reached down and started flapping my tits while I was doing him, and that got even bigger laughs. "Wal, wud'jew lookit *thet!* Pigs reely *dew* have wings!" Another kick in the ass was that some of these crackers had their seedy girlfriends with them, and these chicks pitched a big fit about their boyfriends getting blowjobs from another girl, but when Kezzy—correction, *fuckin'* Kezzy—put $50 bills in their hands, they calmed down fast. Thanks a lot, Kezzy.

One of my guys howled, "Heeeer comes lunch, lard-ass!" when he came, then another guy went, "Cha-ching!" and fired a whopper down my throat. Then this other guy who looked like Jethro on the Beverly Hillbillies whips his out in my face and, I swear, he had *two* pee-holes on his knob, and then there was another guy who I'm pretty sure had three balls.

Big dick, little dicks, bent dicks, sway-back dicks—*every* motherfuckin' kind of dick went in my mouth and blew its load. But I did like I'd been doing, I kept my mind blank and just *did* it, thinking, *Suck and swallow, suck and swallow...*

A lotta my guys were coming real fast, like ten, fifteen seconds, like that. One guy who looked like that guy who was president a long time ago, Clinton, I swear, all I had to give him was one suck down and he came. Couldn't figure it, because it looked to me like Hannah was taking a lot longer to get her guys off. When two hayseed twin brothers put their dicks in my mouth at the same time, five seconds later they were both *coming* at the same time. And I got a lot of pats on the head, too, and one guy, after lasting, like, ten seconds, even said, "Thet theer was the best blow I evuh had'n my life!" I had to ask myself, why are my guys shooting their loads so much faster, and the only answer I could think of was, *Well, I guess that means I give better head.*

How do you like that? I finally found something I do good... or well...or however the fuck you're supposed to say it.

At one point a county sheriff walked in and the place got quiet. I thought, *Thank God! We're saved!* but then the 'necks all started honking again when the cop cut in the line, pulled his dick out, and said, "'Scuse me, boys. Police privilege." Naturally he picked *my* line to cut.

Shit, I don't know. It took maybe three hours to do every guy in the place. But just when I thought we were done, *what* happens?

There's this rumbling sound from outside, and it was so loud that the *floor* was shaking. Me and Hannah just sat there, our fat-rolls jiggling from the rumbling. "What is it, Ann!" she shrieked. "An earthquake?"

"Worse, " I said. "Motorcycles..."

Then in walk *twenty more fuckin' guys.* They were all big fat ZZ Top-looking bastards in leather jackets, chains, boots, beards. They busted their guts when they took at look at me and Hannah. Then they started lining up.

"Miss Kezzy?" I pleaded. "We just did the whole room. Do we have to blow these guys, too?"

She traipsed over, her perfect braless tits swinging in a red-silk halter. She leaned over and brought her face an inch from mine. "Are you looking for the *easy* way out, Ann? Alpha House girls *always* go the extra mile, don't they?" Then she grabbed a big pinch of my cheek. "So if you'd like to be an Alpha House sister...you will suck, and you will *swallow...*"

Hannah was crying outright and I was close to that too. "We have to do it, Hannah," I babbled. "We *have* to..."

And we did.

One of the bikers had *shaved* all his dick hair—even his balls!—and there was one really psycho-looking dude wearing a Nazi helmet, and when he pulled his cock out, he had a *swastika* tattooed on the knob. Then another guy had a bunch of asterisks tattooed on his shaft, so I ask, "What's with the asterisks, man?" and he says, "One fer every bitch I kilt."

Great.

One of 'em even slipped me a twenty. "You blow peter better'n my old lady," he told me and, fuck, I guess I really *did* give great head. But I just kept sucking every dick that got put in my face, and after a while, some of the dicks and sacks started to look *familiar.* Here was Mr. Cheese again, and then came Jethro with the two piss-slits, then Three Balls. *Holy shit!* I thought. *Some of these scumbags are coming back for SECONDS!* But just when the guys left were literally "petering out," I see several of 'em on their cellphones. "Dickie, this is Micky-Mike! Get on down ta Whipple's! Got a pair of fat head-queens blowing every fella in the bar!" and this other shit-head who looks like Willie Nelson jams his dick in my mouth and he's yammering in *his* cell. "Shee-it, Travis! It's Alpha House Pledge Week. Come on down'n bring the crew."

My God. They were calling their friends...

Just didn't seem right but I knew what Kezzy would say if I begged, and sure enough, the place started to fill up again. But by now, me and Hannah were filling up, too, and I started to wonder if a person could actually *die* from sperm poisoning. My stomach was so bloated, I felt like I'd just finished Thanksgiving Dinner, but *this* wasn't turkey. *This* was cum...

Finally, Kezzy came over with her typical evil grin and said, "All right, ladies. That's enough for now."

Me and Hannah were probably both retarded by then. When I got out of my chair to get my clothes, all that cum in my stomach kind of *swayed*, so I lost my footing and fell down. *More* laughter, *more* hee-hawing. The naked fat girl fell, har, har, har.

Kezzy helped me up. "*Do* be careful, Ann. Oh, and now that your work is over for the time being, I suspect that both of you have a certain *burden* you'd like to get shed of?"

"Does she mean we can throw up now?" Hannah whispered to me.

"That's correct, Hannah." Kezzy pointed. "The ladies room is down there."

We *barreled* for the door, banged into it. I got to the toilet first, and all it took was one little push with my finger against the bottom of my tongue, then *all that cum* started to urp up. It took six heaves to get it all out, and since I'd had so little in my stomach to begin with, it tasted like pure sperm coming back out.

"Hurry!" Hannah squealed, and then she did the same. When I looked down into the toilet, I could see that we'd raised the water level by a couple of inches. Half of the cum floated and half of it sunk. It looked like a fuckin' jellyfish sitting in the bowl.

"That's so *much better*," I moaned.

"I'll say."

Edward Lee

We took turns washing our mouths out, but before we could leave, some drunk chick with a Metallica T-shirt, lopsided tits, and zits all over her face comes in and shoves me against the wall.

"Listen, you two disgusting cows!" she yelled. "You can't just waltz in our bar from your fancy college and blow our boy-friends!"

"Sure we can, Dot Face. In fact, we just did," I said but I saw Hannah standing behind her and motioning me. She was swinging the stall door back and forth.

"We're fightin'," the tramp slurred. "And I'm kickin' both your fat asses."

She took a swing but was so drunk she missed completely. I grabbed her ratty hair, pulled her head halfway into the stall and—

WHACK!

Hannah slammed the door right on her head. It was beauti-ful. Thought her eyeballs would pop out Hannah slammed that door so hard. She flopped to the floor, out cold.

"Come on, help me!" I said.

I grabbed one leg and Hannah grabbed the other, and then we dunked her head into the cum-filled toilet. We just kept dunking and I was laughing. After a couple more dunks—

"Ann?"

Another dunk.

"Ann!"

"What?" I snapped.

"Shouldn't, uh, shouldn't we stop?"

I smirked at her after another dunk. The chick was gurgling. "Stop? Why?"

"Well, she could, like, drown, couldn't she?"

I slowed up on the dunking. "Well, I guess you're right. I guess even a shitty, dirty, drunk redneck bitch doesn't deserve to *die*..."

We left her on the floor and split, so I guess that was my good deed for the day. But now that I think of it, if we *had* drowned her in the cum, then would that've really been a *bad* thing? Rednecks are like lawyers: nobody gives a *shit* when you kill one.

I thought that was it and now we could get out of there. Hannah pushed through the crowd ahead of me but, wouldn't you know it? I'm not two steps out of the bathroom when *another* chick is in my face. It's this skanky redneck 'ho with skull tattoos and Black Velvet breath. Christ, where did this trash *come* from? She walked right up and jabbed her finger in my face, and said, "You're a fat pig! You're so fat'n ugly, there oughta be a *law* against you!"

I bit her finger so hard I think my teeth broke the joint, then I grabbed some rube's empty Ice House bottle and conked her right in the noggin. She fell over out cold laying on the peanut-shell-covered floor with her scrawny legs spread, wearing these shitty, dirty flipflops and I could see the bitch even had skull tattoos on her fucking *feet*. Don't know what came over me then, but I just hauled back and kicked her in the cunt like it was a soccer ball. "With any luck, I busted your fuckin' ovaries, did the tax-payers a *big* favor." The 'necks who were left all burst out laughing —

But that's when Hannah started to scream.

The Elvis-looking guy had her down on the floor and was crawling on top of her with his pants down. "Had me enough blowjobs today, ee-yuh-suh. Now I think I'll slop me up some fat pussy."

He pronounced "pussy" as *puss-ahhhhhh*.

Jesus Christ, the guy was about to rape Hannah on the floor and you know what all the people around her did? They formed a circle and started cheering. *Well fuck this*, I thought and I grabbed a cue-stick. If that asshole popped her hymen, then Hannah'd be kicked out. "You ain't sloppin' up nothin'," I said, and —

CRACK!

—I busted that stick right across his back. When he rolled

off her — yowling — I rammed my heel down on his solar plexus, then —

POP!

— stomped on his head and slammed it back against the floor. *That* fucker wouldn't be raping *anyone*.

But you know how rednecks are. A little scuffle turns into a *big* scuffle, and next thing I know, Hannah's fighting with some meth-head chick, and I've got two girls pulling my hair and throwing punches at me. Most of the punches missed 'cos they were so fucked up on drugs and booze, but still. I didn't really need this after blowing a whole bar full of rednecks.

"Chick-fight! Chick-fight! Chick-fight!" everyone started yelling.

"That was my sister you kicked, you fat bitch!" this one hose-bag yells and tries to choke me. I looked over and saw Hannah's boobs flopping up and down while she had two more skinny bitches in headlocks. When she banged their heads together, they were both out like lights.

It was fuckin' *crazy*. *Everybody* was fighting. Now the place looked like one of those dumbass pro wrestling matches where everybody's in the ring at once. But most of the chicks were coming for *me*. First, another meth-head girl started slapping at my fat, and — ooo — I didn't like that shit, so I bit her on the nose and slammed her head down into my knee, but then this *other* bitch with, like, blond hair streaked with purple the color of grape Kool-Aid and — would you believe it? — *skull* tattoos, she pulls a *knife* on me. "My boyfriend Jory said you give better head than me, you fat bitch! Fat, fat, fat! Well, I'm gonna *cut* me some fat now!"

Remember when I said you can only fuck with fat people so long before they lose it? Well, I lost it. I grabbed the hooker's wrist, broke it against a table till she dropped the knife, then threw *all my weight* into her. It was like a Mack Truck running down a stop sign. I tackled her and when we were going down, she cracked her head against the edge of the bar. Out like a light.

Going Monstering

But that wasn't enough for me. I hauled her over the bar belly-down and pulled up her skanky redneck jeans skirt. The 'ho wasn't even wearing panties, but that worked out better. "Hannah! Come over here and spread this bitch's cheeks!" I yelled.

Hannah lumbered over, huffing and puffing. "What are you gonna *do*?"

"Just do it!" I grabbed the soda gun from behind the bar and when Hannah pulled her butt-cheeks open, I popped the nozzle into her asshole and filled the bitch up with Diet Pepsi.

"Wow, that's neat!" Hannah squealed.

Yeah. It was neat, all right. *Real* neat.

But it was that move that did it. Everybody was going even more psycho now — it was a total free-for-all. Dudes were fighting dudes, chicks were fighting chicks, some chicks were fighting dudes and *winning* — even the old bartender was bopping people on the head with a broom. Glasses and bottles were flying, girls' tops were ripped off, tables were being crushed flat. "We gotta get out of here, Hannah!" I yelled. "This is turning into a redneck riot!"

We grabbed our clothes and were about to scoot, but then Hannah asked, "Wait a minute! Where's Kezzy?"

It was a good question 'cos I didn't see her, but then I looked into the billiard room...

"Holy shit!"

Jethro and Willie were mauling Kezzy on the pool table. One had her top pulled down and was motorboating between her boobs, and the other guy was yanking her panties off.

"Stop that!" I screamed. I grabbed Willie by the hair but he just put his hand in my face and shoved me away. I landed on a table and crushed it flat. Hannah helped me up. "We have to get Zenas!" but before we could even get to the front door —

The front door *kicked down.*

The fighting stopped like a freeze-frame, and the whole bar was silent. Then Zenas walked in.

If you thought the uproar was bad before, that was *noth-*

ing compared to this. When these rednecks got a load of Zenas standing there in his maid's suit, they started laughing so hard I thought the ceiling was gonna collapse. But the best part was... they weren't laughing for long.

Zenas kicked off his size-13 pumps, then grabbed Willie and in, like, one second, turned him upside-down, dropped him on his head, and karate-chopped his crotch all in one motion. Even if the guy *didn't* fracture his skull, he'd never have kids, which was a good thing 'cos they'd all be meth-babies anyway. Jethro stood a head taller than Zenas and was even more muscular, but when he slammed his fist into Zenas's face—

Nothing happened.

Zenas just smiled and tossed the guy out the window.

There were still ten or fifteen guys in the bar, though, and these guys were *tough*, but it didn't matter, two against one, three against one, four—shit. Zenas beat the living shit out of all of them. It was like watching a saloon fight in an old John Wayne western flick, only in this case John Wayne was dressed like a fuckin' French maid. In ten minutes, every dude in the place was out cold.

"Jeez, Zenas," I said. "You're a one-man ass-kicking crew."

"Wal, naow, sumtimes a man's gotta take the boys ta school, yew know? En't new big deel."

We found Kezzy at the bar. She was handing the bartender a stack of cash. "For the damage, Mr. Whipple. And thank you for accommodating us."

"Always a pleasure," the old crank said.

We headed for the door but, just my luck, *another* redneck chick with skull tattoos staggers up to me and Hannah and says, "You two fat pieces of shit get *out'a* heer, and don't'jew *never* come back! You en't nothin' but a coupla *whores*, a coupla *big, fat WHORES!*" and the crocked floozy pronounced "whores" as *hoo-ers*.

"Yew're daddy must'a had dogshit on his dick when he knocked yer mamma up with yew," Zenas said and—

Going Monstering

POW!

—socked both of his fists into her eyes and sent her flying.
She landed on a table and, of course, crushed it flat. Even before
she landed, her eyes were puffed closed, and a bunch of crystal
meth flew out of her purse when she hit.

Zenas put his arms around our shoulders and led us out.
"Curn't have no white trash talkin' bad to *Alpha House* gals, new
suh."

Wow. What a cool guy.

We got our clothes back on but before I got back in the car,
I noticed Jethro—the two-holer—lying out cold in the parking
lot.

WHAM!

I kicked him in the dick so hard my foot hurt.

Kezzy frowned at me. "Ann? Why did you do that?"

"Um, well, Miss Kezzy, I did it because I felt like it."

She winked and smiled. "The *honest* answer is always the
only answer. Good girl."

Then we were out of there. I'd have a couple bruises tomorrow, but nothing was broken I didn't think. In all that commotion, though, me and Hannah had forgotten that we'd just
blown every guy in a crowded bar. I know it's all fucked up
but...you know?

How many girls can say they've done that?

"Well, ladies. Congratulations are certainly in order. You've
both passed your Rednecking initiation with flying colors."
She flipped through a little notepad. "I'm sure you were both
so focused on your tasks that it didn't occur to you to keep a
tally, so I kept one for you. Hmm, let's see." She was counting
sets of crossed out lines in the notebook. "Well, Hannah, you
did well—you blew fifty nine men today—but I'm afraid Ann's
bested you considerably..."

I gulped.

She stared at me with her perfect fuckin' blond eyebrows
raised. "Ann. I'm flabbergasted. You may find it gratifying to

know that when *I* was a pledge, I racked up ninety-nine, but you, Ann? *You?*" She nodded at me, the way a father would nod at his son when he hit a home run in Boy's Club. "Today you performed the act of fellatio...*one hundred and eleven times.* Give yourself a pat on the back! You've set the Alpha House *record!*" then everybody started clapping.

How do you like that? For the first time in my life, I finally won something.

A redneck cock-chugging contest.

I just kind of sat back and sighed, feeling damn good. I couldn't wait to get back to the house but when I looked out the Rolls' window I saw that we were heading east.

Away from the house.

"Miss Kezzy? Where are we going now?"

"Don't sit too snugly on your high horses, girls. You both know that there are *two* initiations per day."

Hannah and I gaped at each other. "You mean we have to blow *more* guys somewhere else?" I croaked.

Kezzy pulled something out of a bag up front. "As is often the case in life, there's good news and there's bad news. The good news is that, no, you won't have to blow any more men tonight..."

Then she handed us each a tube of something, like the same size of a tube of toothpaste. Me and Hannah squinted at the tubes to read the labels.

"Oh, noooooooo," Hannah moaned.

The tubes read ANAL EASE.

Kezzy's face was *all* lit up. "The bad news is, tonight you're going Basketball Playering..."

💀 💀 💀

Going Monstering

ARKHAM'S where we went, another *three fuckin' hour* drive, and me and Hannah were practically shitting our pants the whole way. Basketball Playering. For fuck's sake...

It was Miskatonic University we were headed to, some place, Kezzy said, called Gilman Field House, which I guess was the place they played in. Hannah cried a lot, and all I could do was hope that she didn't fold like Mercy. I didn't know much about basketball but I did know that the college seasons didn't start till, like, November or December and, shit, classes hadn't even officially started yet, but then Kezzy reminded me that the teams always started practicing early. Then I tried to argue with the bitch.

"Miss Kezzy? College basketball players are jocks, they're *studs*. Guys like that go out with the best-looking girls on the campus. They aren't gonna want to butt-fuck a couple of fat dogs like me and Hannah."

"Yeah!" Hannah sniffled.

Kezzy was fussing with her lashes. "Ordinarily, no, they wouldn't—not in a *million years*. But since I'll be paying them each a hundred dollars, believe me, they'll be more than happy to oblige just like they do *every* year."

How's *that* for a kick in the ass?

It was dark by the time we got to the basketball court. We could hear the echoes of balls bouncing and guys hooting from inside. "They're at least gonna use rubbers, right, Miss Kezzy?" I asked.

She and Zenas *honked* laughter.

When we parked, Kezzy said, "Here we are, ladies." Hannah just sat there, kind of squished back in the seat, hugging herself.

"I can't do it," she droned.

"Bullshit, Hannah! Don't turn into a baby now!"

She started blubbering. "I can't, I can't! It's just...too much"

I grabbed her and shook her. "We're not pussying out like

Mercy! We're going the whole nine yards! Do you wanna think that you sucked off *fifty-nine* rednecks for *nothing?*"

She looked at me and gulped. "No..."

"Then come on." I tried to sound upbeat. "Don't worry, this'll be a breeze. There's only five guys on a basketball team, so what's the big deal? Look, you take two, I'll take three. Okay?"

"Oh, well... That doesn't sound so bad."

Kezzy kept laughing when she took us into the field house, and I found out why once inside. Turns out there's *twenty-five* guys on a basketball team. "The first string," Kezzy explained, "the second string, the backups, the substitutes." And leave it to that fuckin' evil bitch, she even cut in the towel boys, the managers, and the fuckin' *head coach!* There was even some dude jumping around in a big fluffy bullfrog suit — he was the mascot or some shit.

"Oh, fuck," I said. Hannah about passed out.

The short version? None of these guys were short, and I'm not just talking height. On their *knees* they were taller than us. But when we walked onto the court, they were all cracking up and hollering so loud you'd think they had a championship game going on, and when they pulled their shorts down and hauled off their jock-straps?

I mean, there was not one single kid on the team who wasn't hung.

"Just keep your mind blank, Hannah," I egged on. "We're gonna do this, and we're gonna get *out* of here," but when Kezzy said, "Okay, girls, off with your clothes," I pitched a fit right back in her face. "Why, Miss Kezzy? We always gotta strip, and that ain't right! Can't we at least leave our tops on?"

"No," she said.

"Why?"

"Because I said so, Ann. Don't disappoint me."

"But it's like you're rubbing it in! Having to do it's bad enough! Try being fat and having to take all your clothes off in front of a basketball court full of good-looking guys!"

Going Monstering

She crossed her arms and got back to that foot-tapping thing. "It's necessary for you to be totally naked because it makes the element of debasement more polarizing."

"Debasement! Great! That's what this shit's all *really* about, isn't it?"

"If you believe that, Ann, then you can go wait in the car and leave the house when we get back. Is that what you'd prefer? Hmm?"

I really hated those *hmms*.

"No, Miss Kezzy." I looked and saw all those college kids forming two lines at the foul line, and a lot of 'em were already hard just from *thinking* about how great it was gonna be to dump a load up a fat girl's ass. Eight, nine inches a lot of them looked. But when I saw one dude with a boner even bigger than Zenas's, I pitched another fit. "They're fuckin' hung like dump trucks! It'll be like sticking Lincoln Logs into Tinker Toy holes! At least pull the huge guys out of line! They'll fuckin' rupture our colons!"

Kezzy just stared at me, blank-faced.

"Come on," I said to Hannah and took her out onto the court. We gave each other a squirt of the Anal Ease, got on our hands and knees, and then I yelled, "Bring it on, jocks!"

There's no reason to describe the *rest* of this horror show. All I'll say is me and Hannah each took it up the ass from over twenty young, horny, big-dicked college athletes. After about the first five we couldn't even stay on our hands and knees anymore so we just lay there on our bellies holding hands while the jocks put the blocks to our butts. Naturally, the dude with the dick bigger than Zenas got in *my* line; it felt like he was stuffing a pack of polenta up my ass. And I was lucky enough to get Coach Armitage, and the fucker was old so, of course, it took him ten or so minutes just to come. After a bunch of guys were done, they jogged to the other end of the court and started shooting hoops again. It was so rude. If you're gonna dump a load up my ass, at least say, "Have a nice day" when you're finished.

When everybody'd gotten their nut, I lay there with my cheek pressed to the floor and I could hear Kezzy's heels echoing toward us. "There's only one left, ladies, so you know what that means. Coin toss. Ann? Call it."

"Heads," I mumbled, drooling.

The coin clinked on the court. "Tails. You lose."

Naturally.

But when I heard that last guy walking up, all the other guys on the court started howling laughter and high-fiving, so I looked over my shoulder and saw that it was that doofus mascot in the fluffy frog suit. The motherfucker didn't even take off the suit to cornhole me, he just pulled his dick out a hole in the front and went to town.

"Good news, girls," Kezzy said a couple minutes later. "You're done. Congratulations."

"Hannah, are you still alive?" I slurred.

"I—I don't know..."

"Look at the bright side. We did it."

She kind of croaked a chuckle. "*Yeah...*"

We actually crawled back to our clothes, and it probably took ten minutes to put 'em back on. My butt hurt *so bad* I almost couldn't walk. But when we finally did limp out of the place, the basketball players all gave us a round of applause.

Kezzy chuckled back to the car. "Well. You ladies got filled up from *both* ends today, hmm?"

"We're not cannolies, Miss Kezzy! We're *people!*"

She stopped us and took my arm. "Is that what you think, Ann? You think you're just *people?* Please think again." Her eyes looked huge. "You are *extraordinary* people. Don't ever forget that."

"Home, Zenas," she said when we were back in the car. "And don't dilly-dally. I want my girls *home* and in *bed* without delay. They need their rest."

"Ee-yuh, ma'am."

Going Monstering

That was maybe the weirdest part. Each thing we had to do got worse and worse but whenever we were done, Kezzy would act like she actually *liked* us and that she really *wanted* us in the sorority. Just another one of the things I couldn't figure. Half the time I thought it was pure bullshit, that it was all an act, but other times?

Me and Hannah were kind of half-comatose during the ride back. A big, white moon followed us along the treetops, and the way the car kind of rocked and the tires hummed, it made me feel buzzed sort of. If my butt hadn't hurt so bad, I'd probably even feel content.

I had the same sorts of dreams that night, and heard those same weird words — in Kezzy's voice...

Shub neb hyr'ik eb hyr'k. Ogthrod ai'f geb'l, ee'h yog-sothoth...

☠ ☠ ☠

OUR butts *still* hurt like a motherfucker the next morning when me and Hannah came downstairs. Actually, it was almost noon; we slept late, and I still felt kind of shitty 'cos I hadn't slept good a single night yet in this house.

"I have weird dreams at night," Hannah mentioned, groaning across the foyer.

"Me, too," but for some reason I was afraid to ask her what the dreams were.

I was afraid...they'd be just like mine...

"Well, you girls are certainly looking a bit *drab* this morning," Kezzy said, forking into a big plate of scrambled eggs. The eggs had big chunks of lobster in them.

Hannah yelped when she sat down.

Drab? I thought. "You might feel *drab*, too, Miss Kezzy, if you'd gotten ass-fucked by a fuckin' basketball team."

"Yes, I suppose I would," she said with a great big smile. But then the smile collapsed. "But I didn't, did I?" Then she whistled laughter. "At the very least, I hope you were both able to make a *unique* contribution to the county sewage system last night."

I stared at her. "Yeah, we sure did, Miss Kezzy."

"Your acrimonious tone is actually quite understandable, Ann; you're merely experiencing the Fifth Day Blues. It's common. But don't be weak, ladies. Never lose your confidence."

I yelped when I sat down.

Zenas came out. His maid's suit was *pink* today. He put down two bowls of yogurt.

"Eat up, girls," Kezzy mumbled with her mouth full of lobster and eggs. "You'll want to keep up your energy, hmm?"

I grimaced at my bowl. "Can't we at least have the kind with fruit in it? This is the unflavored crap."

"Does it taste better than sperm, Ann?"

I frowned.

"Good, so don't complain." She shoveled in another forkful of lobster and eggs. "There are people starving in the world, you know, and judging by *your* waistlines, I think it's safe to say that neither of *you* are among them."

Just then? I would've done *anything* to be able to kick her right in her cunt.

"I'm stuffed," Kezzy said after eating half the plate. "Can't eat another bite."

Me and Hannah both stared at her plate. I'm not sure, but I think I was drooling.

"Oh, I'm sorry, girls. How rude of me. Would you like to have the rest of this?

"Yeah!" me and Hannah both yelled.

She sneered. "Fat chance." She handed the plate to Zenas. "I'm finished, Zenas. Scrape the rest into the garbage."

"Shuh thing."

"Why are you busting our chops so bad!" I yelled. "You talk

Going Monstering

to us like we're scum! You talk to us like you *hate* us!"

"I'll forgive your uncouth tirade, Ann. After all, I suppose you both are a bit on edge." Then her shoulders slumped and she sighed. "Believe it or not, cruelty and hostile deportment aren't my forte at all. I don't *hate* either of you. I like you both very much, but I harass you simply because it's my responsibility as the Senior Sorority Sister. If I were all nice and warm and chirpy, I'd be circumventing my obligations. We *can't* have softies here, Ann. We *can't* have mollycoddles."

Mollycoddles. Terrific.

"So you must be *squeezed* to the bursting point, *pushed* to the breaking point. Only then, girls, will I be able to determine that you're both *good enough* to be admitted to Alpha House." She raised her fuckin' *pinkie* when she took a sip of water. "Alpha House is the hardest sorority to get into, but bear in mind, the hardest *deeds* deliver the *best* rewards."

It sounded like a crock of shit. Rah, rah, rah. Go, team, go. Shit. "So what's it going to be today, Miss Kezzy?" I asked. "How many dicks do we have to suck today? How many times do we have to take it in the butt *today?*"

She popped her brow up. "Well, I can't say that I care for your attitude, Ann, but in response to your rather uncivil query, I'm pleased to tell you that *today* there'll be no sodomy at all, and as for fellatio? You will each only have to suck *two dicks.*"

"Two dicks? Is that all, Miss Kezzy?" Hannah said, all excited. "That'll be easy!"

"Not if they're *elephant* dicks," I spat. "Nothing's easy here, Hannah. Each day is harder. She's not gonna let us off the hook and only make us blow two guys. No way." I nodded to myself. "And you know, Miss Kezzy, I wouldn't even be surprised if you really made us do that. Drive us to the fuckin' zoo and make us blow elephants."

Hannah looked terrified. "You're not. Gonna really makes us. Blow *elephants*, are you. Miss Kezzy?"

She laughed. "No, no, don't be so morbid!"

At least that loosened us up a little. Hannah started drinking her water and I ate some more yogurt —

"Not elephants," Kezzy added. "Chimps."

Hannah hacked on her water and flopped out of her chair, and I spat a mouthful of yogurt clear across the kitchen.

"Chimps?" I yelled. "You mean, like, *monkeys?*"

"Indeed, Ann. Today you and Hannah will be 'Chimping.'"

I could feel my face turn red. "We have to blow *monkeys?*"

"Yes, but we won't be driving you to the *fuckin'* zoo," as you've so pristinely suspected. Today, the fuckin' zoo comes to us," and then we heard a loud rumbling outside. "Ah. That must be them now."

Me and Hannah ran to the window...

A big white truck, like a UPS truck only longer, had just pulled into the front of the house. Letters on the side read KINGSPORT ZOO.

"You've gotta be shitting me!" I yelled.

Hannah opened her mouth, looked at me, then started crying.

"The sooner, the better, ladies," Kezzy said and took us out.

Two guys in gray jumpsuits stood behind the truck, smoking cigarettes and laughing.

Hannah jabbered, "Are there really, are there really..."

"Monkeys in the truck?" I blurted. "You bet your ass, and we have to blow 'em."

Hannah started to gag. "I can't!

Neither can I, I thought, *but I'm gonna do it anyway. I'm not gonna let that sick bitch break me.* I practically dragged Hannah down the driveway. "Listen. It's just two chimps, Hannah. You know, little chim-chim things two feet tall, like what you see on TV. Shit, the other day you blew a German Shepherd and I blew a fuckin' Great Dane. This'll be easy compared to that."

"No it won't!" she wailed.

I grabbed her hard by the shoulders and glared at her. "We can't let Kezzy break us," I hissed at her. "We've been doing awful shit all week, but if we don't do this, then it's all for nothing. That means we blew old men, bums, dogs, and a shit-hole bar full of rednecks and then got butt-fucked by a basketball team for *nothing!*

"I know, but-but—"

"*Think* about it, Hannah. There's only *two more days to go!* We're almost there! Don't make me do this by myself."

"Well," she sniffled.

"We do like we been doing all week. We keep our minds blank, don't think about anything, just detach ourselves from what it really is. We won't think, *Oh, fuck, I'm sucking a monkey's dick,* we think *nothing*. Now come on," and then I pulled her toward the back of the truck. "We'll blow the little buggers and be done with it."

The two assholes from the zoo were honking when they helped us up a little ladder. Kezzy followed. I could smell the things before I even looked into the back of the truck, but then I *did* look into the back of the truck...

"Those aren't chimps!" I yelled. "They're fuckin' *gorillas!*"

Serious. They had the two monkeys' hairy arms and legs chained upright to a metal rack. Little buggers? Chim-chims?

My ass. These things were fuckin' taller than me.

Overhead lights snapped on, then the two guys from the zoo pulled the back door down.

"Ann, Hannah," Kezzy said. "I'd like you to meet Buddy and Ollie. And don't be deceived, they're not gorillas, they're full-grown chimps of the mammalian classification Pan *Troglodytes*. The little 'chim-chims' you were thinking of are *Pan Paniscus* — *pygmy chimpanzees*..."

"That's really terrific, Miss Kezzy," I said, staring at these terrifying motherfuckers. I mean, they had gray beards and *fangs*. Then Kezzy told us they were *forty-five years old!* When the things saw us, their eyes jacked open and they howled.

Hannah and I screamed.

"If they break those chains, they'll kill us!"

Going Monstering

"Naw," one of the guys said. "These chimps are about three times stronger than the strongest man, but that's 2000-pound test chain. Ain't no way they can bust it, and even if they did, they probably wouldn't kill ya."

"Yeah," the other guy laughed, "but they'd sure as shit *fuck* ya!"

"Chop-chop, girls," Kezzy said. "Oh, and off with your clothes."

"Bullshit! I'm not stripping for monkeys!"

Kezzy shrugged. "Fine. Then leave. Shall I call you a cab?"

Oh my God, I thought.

"Chimps get excited by the sight of naked human females," the bitch added. "They'll be more accommodating if they're happy."

Moaning, me and Hannah stripped, and when we were both nude, the things—Buddy and Ollie, for fuck's sake—started howling again and wouldn't stop. They were already pulling boners! *Think positive, think positive*, I kept telling myself

"And, my God, they *stink!*" Hannah bawled.

"Aw, shit, Hannah, they don't smell as bad as those bums the other night, and probably half those rednecks," I mumbled. "And, look. Their dicks are *tiny.*"

"Wonderful!" Kezzy said. "Always looking at the bright side. A positive outlook will always forge a better future. Hannah, you should take a lesson from Ann. With Ann, the cup is always half-full, not half-empty. Her observation is quite correct. A chimpanzee erection averages eight centimeters, that's about three and a half inches."

I elbowed Hannah. "See. This won't be so bad."

"And their typical seminal discharge is only a third of the average man's—oh, and you'll both be happy to know that chimps tend to achieve orgasm after only about nine seconds of direct stimulation."

"We can do this, piece of cake," I said.

But then Kezzy said, "*That's* the good news."

Me and Hannah glared at her.

"The bad news is, though chimps *come* quickly, they also *refract* quickly."

"What the hell's that mean?" I snapped.

"The average *Pan Troglodytes*, after achieving orgasm, has the ability to regain erectile and ejaculatory competence in less than a minute. We can't let you ladies off too easily, now can we? That is why you'll each be required to blow your chimp *three times*."

Hannah wailed, but I thought, *It just gets sicker and sicker.*

"Come on," I told Hannah and pulled her toward the back. "Come on-come-on-come-on!" and when we got closer, the chimps started howling so loud it sounded like we were in the middle of a fuckin' jungle. I guess the one I got was Ollie — fuck. I just got down on my knees and started sucking its pecker, and once I did that, Hannah started too. It wasn't so bad — at least not as bad as you'd *think* blowing a monkey would be — kind of like sucking back and forth on half a Slim Jim, but I'll tell you, the second the monkeys had their dicks in our mouths, they went crazy with these "ooo-ooo-ooo" sounds. Kezzy wasn't kidding about coming fast, either. After six or seven sucks on Ollie's little tool, he shot his load in my mouth. Tasted pretty much like a guy's jizz, I guess. I counted to three, swallowed it, then started sucking again. While I was doing it, I side-glanced over to Hannah, and when Buddy came, her head snapped back and she brought her hand to her mouth with her eyes squeezed shut. I guess that was when the reality hit her, *Oh, shit, I've got chimp cum in my mouth,* and then her stomach started sucking in and out.

"Don't spit it out!" I yelled.

Kezzy was tapping her foot again. "You know the rule, Hannah. After you suck, what do you do? You *swallow*."

She doubled over, tears plipping out of her eyes, but eventually she just bucked up, gulped it down, and got back to business. "Good girl," Kezzy said, but the two guys from the zoo were doubled over worse than she'd been, they were laughing so hard.

It wasn't more than another thirty seconds before Ollie blew in my mouth again, then another maybe minute and a half to get him off the third time. *Down the hatch,* I thought and swallowed the last one. Hannah got her second nut too, but then it looked like she sucked another couple more minutes and Number Three still hadn't happened.

"Why, Ann," Kezzy said, "Ollie there seems to be enamored of you."

I looked up at Ollie's horrific fanged monkey face, and it was actually making kissy-face at me, and worse...

His little boner was up in full force again.

"You're a compassionate person, Ann. Wouldn't it be nice to give Ollie another blowjob out of the simple goodness of your heart?"

"No, it would fuckin' not, Miss Kezzy!" I wasn't even thinking about the fact that I had monkey sperm in my stomach, I was thinking about how *much* I hated her. "I'll tell you what, I'll blow Ollie again, if you blow him first. How's that for a deal? *Hmmmmmmmmmmmm?*"

God, it felt so good to do that.

"It doesn't work that way, Ann, but I'll give you credit for trying," she said.

Meanwhile, Hannah's head was whipping back and forth on Buddy's chimp-dick, and then she started whining.

"Come on," I complained. "Get the fuckin' monkey off so we can get *out* of this zoo on wheels."

Another minute and she stopped and looked over. "He's not coming, Ann! I think, I think he's doing it on purpose!"

"Just like a man," Kezzy chuckled.

"Gimme a break, Hannah! Jeez, you're worse than Mercy!"

"Ann, you're the resourceful one," Kezzy said. "And let me remind you that, like male humans, male *chimps*, too, are possessed of prostate glands."

I just kind of slumped there on my knees. *Why me?* I wondered.

Hannah broke down. "I can't! I just *can't*, Ann! I can't stick my finger up a monkey's ass! Please! Do it for me?"

I put my face in my hands and groaned.

"Feeling sporting today, Ann?" Kezzy said. "*I* am. How about this? We'll flip a coin. You lose, *you* stick your finger up Buddy's ass. But if you win?" She grinned. "*I* will."

My eyes *darted* to her prissy Fifth Avenue face. Seriously, if I had a million bucks, I'd pay it to see Kezzy finger a chimp's ass. But...

"I always lose the toss," I groaned.

"Come on, Ann!" Hannah rooted. "You've lost every coin toss so far. The odds have to be in your favor!"

"Though Hannah is *hardly* a statistician, she's got a pertinent point," Kezzy said.

I started sweating and wringing my hands. The chimps were "ooo-ooo-ooo"ing, and the zoo guys were still laughing.

I gulped. "Deal."

Kezzy handed me a quarter. Just a regular quarter, not a trick one.

"*You* call it," I said and flipped it up...

"Tails," Kezzy said.

The coin chinked on the metal floor and spun around. Seemed like it spun around a whole minute. Then it fell over.

Tails.

Kezzy *squealed* laughter.

I didn't even bother getting mad. Why? I walked over on my knees, spat on my finger, and stuck it right up Buddy's chimpanzee asshole. All it took was a few more sucks from Hannah, and Buddy came...

Even Kezzy had tears in her eyes from laughing so hard. She passed wads of cash to the zoo guys while me and Hannah got dressed. The chimps kept hooting and clacking their chains. They were obviously pissed that we were leaving.

Going Monstering

"Ann!" Kezzy said with a raised brow. "Your invidiousness is quite alarming."

I gaped at her. "My *what?*"

"Your lack of *fairness.*"

"Missy Kezzy, I don't know what the FUCK you're talking about."

She pointed to Buddy, who kept "ooo"ing and staring at me. "Chimps are the closest life form to human beings — they have intuition, self-awareness, the ability to calculate and... They have *feelings*, Ann."

"So what?" I yelled.

"How would you feel if, for instance, I gave Hannah a New Zealand lobster tail for dinner but not you?"

"I'd be so fuckin' pissed off I'd kick a hole in the fuckin' wall."

"Then how do you think Buddy feels?" She tapped her fuckin' foot. "You just put your finger up *Ollie's* ass — it's only fair that you now put your finger up *Buddy's* ass, hmm?"

I pictured myself strangling Kezzy very slowly with piano wire. "The only thing I'd ever want to put up Buddy's ass is maybe a fuckin' banana loaded with rat poison. Make the fucker croak and go to fuckin' Monkey Hell," and then I strode past her. The lead zoo guy rolled the truck door back up, and then me and Hannah came down the ladder.

"Ann? Hannah? Where are your manners?" Kezzy had a scolding look. "Aren't you even going to say goodbye to Buddy and Ollie?"

"*Fuck* Buddy and Ollie," I grumbled. "Send 'em to fuckin' Africa where they belong. Maybe they'll get eaten by lions or pythons or something."

And when I got to the bottom step?

I tripped and fell.

Another laugh riot.

"'Bye, girls," said the one zoo guy with a big grin. "Thanks for the entertainment. I'll tell ya, watching two fat girls blow chimps is tough to beat."

"Fuck off," I said, then me and Hannah walked back up to the house, but before we were halfway there, a big commotion broke out in the truck. I heard the chimps going nuts and chains thrashing, and then—

One of the zoo guys started screaming bloody murder.

The other zoo guy jumped down from the truck. He had *blood* on his face.

"Run!" he yelled at us. "The chimps went nuts when you left, so they broke their chains and killed Wally! Run for your lives!"

Me and Hannah both pissed our pants in sheer terror 'cos we knew those chimps were coming for us. *They'll fuck us silly!* I thought. Hannah was blubbering. "Go! Go!" I screamed. "Open the door!"

When we finally got to the front door, I dared to look back at the truck. I just *knew* I'd see Buddy and Ollie apeing their way after us, "ooo-ooo-ooo"ing with their little dicks hard, but...

Kezzy and the two zoo guys were doubled over again laughing.

"Only kidding, girls," the one dude said while he wiped the ketchup off his face.

Me and Hannah both started crying.

After puking up the chimp sperm into the toilet, we showered and changed, and I scrubbed my finger with every different kind of soap and disinfectant I could find. Hannah had this crazy look in her eyes, she stalked around the room opening and closing her fists and kicking stuff. "I can't take it! I can't take it anymore! I can't take it!"

"We got the job done, Hannah, so don't go apeshit."

"Oh, you would say *apeshit!*" she yelled.

I wagged my finger at her. "*I'm* the one with apeshit on her finger, so quit complaining. You're forgetting the most important part. We're almost *done* with initiations. Just a few more hazes and we're *in*."

Going Monstering

She sat down on her bunk and calmed down. "Well, yeah. You're right."

I sniffed my finger and howled. Ollie's stink just wasn't coming all the way off. I found a bottle of Clorox under the sink and soaked my finger in it.

Zenas walked right in. This time the maid's suit was baby-blue with yellow fringe, and he wore blue high heels.

"Thanks for knocking," I said.

He sniffed the air. "I'se *swear* I smell another asshole finger in heer."

"Fuck off."

"Git'cher fat asses downstairs, both'a yew," he said. "Yer stylists are heer."

Stylists?

Downstairs, two swishy looking dudes in black-silk shirts and white slacks were waiting. "Ladies," the fussy blond one said in a French accent, "I am Jacques, and theese eese Gilles." They sat us down in the living room chairs and had all their hair-styling gear set up.

"What's this all about?" I asked.

"Ooo, just you wait, my pretty plump one," Jacques said. "I make you beau-tee-ful."

The last thing I needed was some French fag calling me his "pretty plump one," but by then I was too tired and shocked to say a thing. An hour later, though—

"Holy shit" we both said then they held mirrors up.

Our hair looked *great!* My hair's been a rat's nest my whole life: thick, dry, sticking all over the place but, now? I had movie-star hair and so did Hannah. After that, two Asian girls did our nails, then a third French guy took our measurements. When I asked him who he was, he said, "My name eese Claude; I am your wardrobist."

We didn't know what was going on. Why was Kezzy getting us gussied up? When I asked her later, she said, "I'm getting you girls *prettified* for your induction, Ann."

Edward Lee

"But, Miss Kezzy," Hannah asked. "Don't we still have more initiations to pass?"

"Yes, but only two. You've completed everything so far — I've complete confidence that you'll both be inducted."

She said it, like, real casually, like it was no big deal, but to me and Hannah it was the biggest deal of our lives. We both walked around in the backyard for the next hour, all giddy and lit up. Then that Claude dude called us in.

This guy *made* two evening dresses for us. They were black and kind of glittery. Silk nylons, necklaces, classy high heels, too. I almost shit when I looked in the mirror.

"I've never looked so good in my life!" Hannah was almost crying.

"Me, either. Shit. For two fat girls, we look damn good, but—"

Then we both looked at each other.

Then Kezzy called us down.

"My, what an elegant duo you ladies are," Kezzy said. She was all gussied up, too, and looked a million, no, a *trillion* times better than we did, but so what? This was the best I'd *ever* looked.

But the question itched at us.

"Miss Kezzy? It's Thursday night. Induction isn't till Saturday. What gives with the makeovers?"

Kezzy smirked. "What *gives*, Ann, is the necessity for the two of you to look good tonight. For your second to last hazing."

Time seemed to stand still until one of us—I don't even know which—asked, "What...do we have to do?"

"Tonight, girls," Kezzy said, "you'll be going Fathering."

A long pause. "Fathering?" Hannah asked.

"Yes, Hannah."

"Fathering?" I asked, "As in...*what?*"

"Think about it, Ann."

"We have to blow our *fathers?*" I half-shouted.

Kezzy nodded. "Precisely."

Going Monstering

I laughed out loud. "Well, that's gonna be a trick 'cos my father lives in D.C. and Hannah's lives in Dallas. What? Zenas is gonna *drive* us there?"

Just then, car doors thunked outside. Kezzy looked out the window. "Ah, here's Zenas now, just back from the airport." She turned, with her hands clasped, then tapped her foot. "With your parents..."

💀 💀 💀

HOW do you like *that* shit? She invited our parents to come here to see the sorority house and have fuckin' *dinner* with us! That was bad enough, but the part I didn't get at all was the "Fathering" deal. How on *earth* could she make us blow our *fathers?*

We didn't have time to ask 'cos Kezzy was opening the door and inviting them in a second later.

Of course, Zenas wasn't in the maid suit this time, he wore a regular guy suit, and when my parents saw me, I thought they would keel over. "Oh, Ann, dear!" my mother wailed and hugged me. "You look *marvelous!*"

"And you've lost weight," my father said.

"And so have you, Hannah!" her mother squealed.

"Your daughters are getting accustomed to Alpha House discipline," Kezzy said. "Here at Alpha House we have a formidable exercise and nutritional regimen, which Ann and Hannah have taken to with great enthusiasm."

Hannah and I both wanted to hurl. The only exercise we'd had was moving rocks, sucking dick, and taking it up the ass. And the nutritional regimen? Yogurt, pretzel rods, and cum. No fuckin' *wonder* we'd lost some weight.

Kezzy's lashes just kept batting over the light-up-the-room

smile. "Mr. and Mrs. White? Mrs. and Mrs. Bowen? You should congratulate yourselves for raising such bright, motivated, and disciplined daughters."

What a crock of shit. She was probably just buttering them up for a contribution. But my mother was so overjoyed to hear somebody say something *positive* about me, she had tears in her eyes. She gave me another hug and a big, wet kiss on the cheek. "I'm so proud of you, honey."

"Thanks, mom."

"Didn't think you had it in you," my father said. The *fuck*. After all the introductions were finished, then Zenas came in with a tray of fuckin' brandy snifters. The rich farts really dug that. Louis the something or other, it was called. Then Kezzy took us all around the house to give our parents a tour, chatterboxing away the whole time.

Hannah's parents were stuck-up fucks, just like mine, but maybe a little older, like fifty. Her father was one of those shyster CEO's who bilked the shit out of some big banking institution, then ran it into bankruptcy, and walked away with, like, $30 million of severance pay. Looked like a used car dealer, though; just another scumbag in an expensive suit with "distinguished" gray temples; and her mother was just kind of a jowly, fat priss with Betty Crocker hair. But my parents were in their forties and kind of good-looking, I guess. Dad looked George Clooneyish and mom could've been on any of those *Sex in the City*-type shows that always kind of made me fuckin' sick. She had the implants, the tummy tucks, the salon tan. Rich assholes like this were hard to impress but, believe me, both my parents and Hannah's were *really* impressed by the fancy sorority house and the refined, high-class Kezzy who they believed was going to magically transform their lazy slug daughters into well-bred college grads with shining futures.

"'Scuse me, folks," Zenas said after the house-tour. "Dinner is served." The group started to move toward the dining room but then my father pulled me aside.

Going Monstering

"Ann. I don't know what to say. This isn't a joke, is it?"

"What do you mean, dad?"

"Well, it sounds like one of those things that's too good to be true."

I smoldered to myself. "Because you can't believe that your no-account daughter is actually succeeding in something? Thanks a lot, dad."

His voice hardened. "That's not what I meant, and I'll do without that typical smart-ass tone. After all your fuck-ups, how can you *not* expect me to be a little suspicious?"

I just shrugged.

"This house is magnificent, and Kezzy couldn't be more squared away—"

You just like her tits, you phony creep, I thought.

"And there's nothing I'd like more than to see her put you on the right path."

It was hard not to crack a smile. *Today I sucked off a chimp named Buddy*, I thought. *How's that for the "right path?"*

"She mailed us the Alpha House brochure, and it said that every single Alpha House girl to graduate from this college since the 1700's did so with academic *honors. Every single one.* So I thought, *bullshit*, and I had my research department check it out."

"And?"

He looked thrown for a loop. "It's all true. And then I think to myself, what's wrong with this picture? Am I being *harsh* in, frankly, not having any confidence in you? Am I an *asshole* for believing that you could *never* be part of such outstanding company? Considering the past?"

I gulped. Just then I either wanted to hang myself right in front of him, or blow his head off. I know I'm a loser, but maybe I wouldn't be if once, just once, my own fucking father would have some confidence in me...

"Oh, don't give me that 'Oh, poor me, my father talks so mean to me' look," he said. "I've seen you in action, Ann, for your whole life, and it's just been one fuck up after the next, disappointment after disappointment, and you *know* it." He looked at me like I didn't have a head. "Are you *really* going to make it into this sorority?"

"I'm going to do everything in my power," I said.

"I hope those aren't just words, Ann." His face looked like a stone mask. "Because if they are?"

He didn't have to finish. I'd be *disowned.*

"Now let's go to dinner," he said and propped up his phony smile and led me into the dining room.

I didn't cry even though I wanted to. I didn't think it was possible to feel *this much* like a useless piece of shit, but that's what I had to hand to my father. He was real good at it.

Dinner was ridiculous, like something at the Mayflower Hotel. Fancy wine, Caesar salad that Zenas prepared tableside, then scallops grilled in pistachio oil, and Beef Wellington. But when Zenas gave me and Hannah yogurt in fancy little silver bowls, Kezzy said, "Ann and Hannah were given the choice of partaking in the same menu as the rest of us, but they elected to stick to their healthy dietetic menu."

Oh, DID we, now? But it didn't matter. I'd forgotten what good food tasted like, and I wasn't even hungry then either 'cos my father made me so sick.

Kezzy was the perfect host, telling our parents more about the college's history and all the great success stories to come out of Alpha House. By the time the Bananas Foster dessert was served they were all good and crocked, and starting to show their true colors. The mothers were gabbing about their designer labels and the fathers were honking about new ways to rip off honest people. But the whole time, me and Hannah were squeezing each others hands under the able, thinking *How the FUCK is Kezzy gonna pull this off?*

When the after dinner coffee was served, we found out.

They were all gabbing away when—clunk, clunk, clunk, clunk—our parents went face down into the table.

"What happened!" Hannah squealed.

But I knew. "Kezzy drugged them."

"As has been the case for the majority of the week," Kezzy said, "yes, Ann. You're correct. Flunitrazepam, also known as Rohypnol, is a quality hypnotic and amnestic sedative which produces semi-unconsciousness."

"She roofied our parents," I said. "I should've known."

"You mean, like that date-rape drug?" Hannah asked, appalled.

"Yes, Hannah, and yet while Flunitrazepam sufficiently inhibits the central nervous system it has only a minimal effect on the *libidinal* nerves; in other words, *sexual* nerve-conduction. And for a little extra ooomf, we've added some good ole Viagra." Kezzy was almost shaking with excitement. "Zenas? Mr. White and Mr. Bowen need to be tactically arranged."

Zenas grabbed both men by the collar and dragged them out to the middle of the living room. Then he pulled their pants down.

Kezzy's grin was almost blinding. "Pretty twisted, huh, ladies?"

"Yeah, it's twisted, all right, Miss Kezzy," I said. "'Fathering.' Only you could think of that."

"Oh my God, oh my God, oh my God!" Hannah said.

"Ladies?" Kezzy clapped her hands once. "Suck and swallow..."

For fuck's sake. We both walked into the living room like two girls walking to the gallows. Dad's pants and shorts were pulled all the way down to his ankles; he was wearing black socks up to his knees. This was the first time I ever saw my father's cock, and guess what?

It was big.

"Let's see some real Alpha House spirit, okay, girls?" Kezzy said. "I want you to blow your fathers with *zeal*."

"Great," I said—whatever *zeal* meant—and got down on my knees. And then?

I started sucking my father's dick...

I guess it could've been worse—it wasn't *quite* as big a Zenas's. It got hard real fast, so I just started going 'cos the faster I got him off, the sooner I'd be able to stop, but then Kezzy tapped me on the shoulder. "A rushed job, Ann, is a *poor* job," she said. "*Slow*, girls, and *meticulous*. They are your fathers, after all."

Dad was leaking some bigtime pre-cum. Then Kezzy said, "Lower, Ann. You've heard the term *deep throat?* I'd like to see some *expert* fellatio."

Wonderful. Now I was practically *inhaling* my father's cock. I glanced over and saw Kezzy with her hands on her knees, and she was leaning over Hannah and Mr. Bowen to watch. "My, Hannah. I see *your* father's not exactly well-equipped in the genital department, hmm?" but Hannah just kept crying even with her father's dick in her mouth.

I kept sucking, then—

"Holy shit! Miss Kezzy!"

See, while I was doing it, dad started mumbling and grabbed my head! "Good lord, Elisa"—my mother's name was Elisa—"you haven't sucked me off like that in years..." and then I looked up and saw his *eyes* open. He was *looking* at me!

"Kezzy, he's *conscious!* He can *see* me!"

"Relax, Ann." Now Kezzy was sitting on the couch, watching. "He's only about ten-percent conscious, but because of Rohypnol's powerful amnesic effect, he won't remember a thing in the morning. None of them will." I guess that's the part that made it even creepier. Not only was I sucking my father's dick, but he was *watching* me, and a minute later he started to mumble again. "Wuh-wait—you're not my wife... *Ann?* Is that you?"

"Yeah, dad, and that's right, I'm sucking your dick, but don't worry, you won't remember."

"Oh... That's nice..."

When dad started moaning, *Kezzy* started moaning, too, and when I looked up, there she was with her classy skirt hiked up, playing with herself. Watching two girls blow their fathers *turned her on*, and when she came, I thought a fuckin' tea kettle was going off. Hannah's old man came so she kind of jerked upright and mumbled with a mouthful of cum, "Oh my God, oh my God, oh my God!"

"Swallow now, Hannah."

She gulped, then started bawling full force.

But I was the one gulping next 'cos my own dad came, and he put five of six good-sized jolts in my mouth. "Good, good!" Kezzy whispered. "Excellent. And what do we do now, Ann?"

I swallowed.

"Very, very good, ladies," she congratulated us. "You've both just passed your *second to last initiation!* I'm *so* proud!"

Hannah just kept bawling. "I-I-I...I just sucked my father's dick!"

"Indeed you have. And you did a *fine* job." Kezzy stood up and patted out her dress. "And in the morning, your parents will wake up—with considerable hangovers, mind you—and not remember *any* of what went on. Then I'll explain to them that they merely over-imbibed." She nodded at both of us, and there really *was* pride in her eyes. "Now, girls, pull your father's pants back up. You're done for the night."

After I got his belt re-done, I rushed to the bathroom to gargle. The taste of cum is bad enough, but your *father's* cum? The same DNA that made *me* was now in *my* stomach. Just knowing that gave me the creeps. Then I went out to the kitchen for a bottle of water but—

"Aw, come on, Zenas!" I bellowed.

Zenas had my mother laid out buck naked on the dining room table. He was standing up at the table edge and had her knees pushed back in her face, and he was still fully dressed in his suit—only his cock and balls were out. Mom's fifty-grand implants jiggled with each stroke. He was fucking her hell for leather.

"What's got'cher dander up, fattie?"

"My *dander?*" I wailed. *"You're fucking my mother!"*

"Wal... Ee-yuh, I'se am. It'd seem a waste not tew." He patted her belly. "Yer ma's got some serious milf goin' on heer. Dynamite tits'n legs, killer ass, and her box is just purdy as a picture." He shot a thumb toward Hannah's mother who was still slumped face-down on the table, her overloaded makeup smearing the tablecloth. "That 'un theer's fat as a Berkshire hog and's got a face like that Joker fella on the Batman movie. "But yer ma?" He whistled. "Mmm-MMM!" and then he started going at it again. He patted her pubis while he was stroking. "And lookit, I say *lookit* this cut on her. *Smooooth.* Just like a baby's butt. Not even no stubble!"

"It's laser hair-removal, Zenas! For shit's sake! Would you *please* stop fucking my mother!"

"Aw, shuh, I'll'se stop fuckin' her after my dick spits." He gave me a cockeyed look, then shot his hand at me and grabbed my hair. "Come over heer a sec, fattie." His hand twisted my hair and forced my face down...

"Yew know, I'se just tickled pink by the ideer'a you lickin' yer ma's puss while I'se plowin' her poon," and then he twisted harder till I squealed and had no choice but to wrench my face down there and start licking. That laser hair-removal is something, though; Zenas was right. No stubble, no nothing.

"Lick like ya mean it," he said next and pushed my head. But I just did like I been doing all week. I made my mind go blank and just *did* the job.

Mom started moaning and murmuring, then, and her ass was squirming. "Henry, Henry, *honey,*" she slurred—my father's name was Henry—"that just feels *wonderful,*" and then her hands were in my hair too. She started hissing then, and fidgeting and arching her back, and then she came even louder than Kezzy.

"'S'awright, fattie," Zenas said and shoved my face away. "Ee-yuh. Juss like they say at the Exxon—fill 'er *up!*"

"That's terrific, Zenas," I said and wiped my mouth off on

117

the tablecloth.

He chuckled, humping hard now. "Curn't figure it, though. I look at her'n I look at yer pa, and I think, wheer the *hail* did *yew* come from. You shuh yew wurn't *adopted* from some fat couple?"

"I really appreciate that."

When Kezzy walked in, she clasped her hands together and squealed in delight. "Oh, this is *just* so wonderful! Ann, you'll be pleased to know that Alpha House has *never* had a better Fathering session than this!"

I turned to leave—one thing I did *not* need to see was some fucked-up redneck getting off in my mother—but before I made it out of there, Zenas said, "Hey, fattie, wait a sec. Wouldn't it be sumpin' if'n *I knocked yer momma up?* Guess that'd make *my* kid *yew're* sister, huh?" and then he and Kezzy laughed like hyenas.

I went upstairs and went to bed.

☠ ☠ ☠

TOMORROW would be Friday, the final day of hazing, and if I made it, I'd be officially inducted into Alpha House on Saturday. It wasn't the suspense of it all that prevented me from sleeping, and it wasn't fear, either. Whatever the final hazes were, they couldn't be any more fucked up than the stuff I'd already done. After a certain point, you realize you simply can't be debased any more. *I sucked my father's cock today,* I realized, *and I went down on my own mother. If I can do that...*

I could do *anything.*

No, the reason I couldn't sleep that night was 'cos I was afraid of those dreams again, those nightmares. The ghost of Joseph Corwan fucking with me, then Zenas spitting in my mouth or making me eat his snot, then Kezzy sitting on my face, then...

Then those *words*...

The words, for some reason, were the worst part.

It was around two when I said fuck it and got up. No way I could sleep so I walked around the house. I peeked into one of the guest rooms and saw mom and dad sleeping. Both had smiles on their faces. *Christ*... Downstairs I got a drink of water, then caught myself looking at the Corwan portrait again, and the brass plate that looked *new* while the frame and painting itself was real *old*. *Why would I have dreams about THIS guy?* I wondered, and I also wondered what his relation was to the other dude — *Curwen* — who founded the college decades later. When I looked out the kitchen window I half-expected to see Kezzy there, naked and reading from that book in candlelight like that first night, but the gazebo was dark.

I moseyed around some more, then wound up back upstairs. I peeked in Kezzy's room but she wasn't in bed...

I thought I heard something then, a soft voice, but wasn't sure, but then I heard it better when I put my ear to the door to the library. Kezzy must've seen my feet in the gap under the door. Louder, she said, "Come in, Ann," and I hadn't even knocked.

The library was long and full of rows of bookshelves. Kezzy, in her Victoria's Secret nightie, sat at a big, angled desk with a bunch of candles lit.

"Can't sleep?"

"No, Miss Kezzy. I guess I'm kind of freaked knowing that my parents are here, and, well — "

She smiled without looking at me. She was reading that big book. "You know you're getting close to induction. It's an exciting time, and please know that I share in your excitement. You did very well today."

I blew my father and went down on my mother...and she's complimenting me, I thought. It was almost funny.

"And I'm sure that you know by now the reason for all of these rather, um, *grievous* acts that you're required to perform," she said, still skimming the book. "It's not merely to make you feel debased and degraded. It's to test your mettle, Ann. By determining, through the engagement of your own free will, to *allow* yourself to be debased and degraded, you demonstrate your...*what*, Ann? *What* do you demonstrate by submitting to such acts?"

"My resolve," I said.

"Precisely."

But was it really my resolve, or just my desperation?

"You're very, very close to becoming an Alpha Sister, Ann. Very few have the resolve to do what you and Hannah have done."

Very, very close? She was right but then—fuck—I started *crying*. Don't know why, it just happened. Instant waterworks right there in front of Kezzy. She was the last person I wanted to break down in front of.

"Ann! Whatever is the matter?"

"Oh, I don't know, Miss Kezzy," I sobbed, "I just think I'm going to wind up getting screwed like I always do, like even when I pass the last hazing, there'll still be some reason I won't get inducted. Nothing *good* ever happens to me..."

"But *great* things are about to happen, Ann. You must believe this."

I just kept crying. "I must be out of my fuckin' mind thinking I can be an Alpha girl."

"Ann. You practically *are* an Alpha girl—"

"Oh, come on! I've seen Alpha girls! I talked to some at orientation last summer. They're all like you, they're all really pretty, and they all get great grades. *I* can't get good grades! *I'll* never be pretty!"

"Ann, I've explained the sorority's fitness plan and tutoring program—"

"Aw, shit, Miss Kezzy. Who am I fooling? I'll never be able to do any of that. All the tutors in the world won't make me smart, because I'm *not* smart, and I could diet and exercise for a hundred years and I'd *still* be fat! Stuff like that never works for

120

me. You know," I sniffled. "My motherfuckin' asshole father is right.. What's wrong with this picture? *Me.*"

Kezzy gave me some tissues. "Come with me." Then put her arm around me and took me down one of the aisles between the bookshelves. One of the sets of shelves was full of books that each had a year printed on the spine. "These are the Alpha files, Ann. They go all the way back to the 1700's, but *here...*" She took a book down. "Here are the most recent ones." The year printed on the cover was three years ago. She opened it and handed me a big photograph. It showed four girls standing in front of Alpha House, all smiling.

They were also all overweight and unattractive.

"The girl on the far left is me," Kezzy said.

Holy shit... My knees went rubbery; I may have actually gotten light-headed by what she'd said. The girl on the left was *huge*, had me by a hundred pounds. But the more I looked at her balloon-face...

The more I saw the resemblance.

"I can't believe what I'm seeing, but..it is you, isn't it?"

"Indeed. I weighed 260, 270 back then, the beginning of my freshman year. And here's my last high school report card." She handed me the printout.

"A one-point-*zero* grade point average?" I said, staring at the grades.

"I was a *terrible* student, Ann—much worse than you. I just never had an aptitude for anything, and never had enough confidence in myself to find one." She handed me another sheet. "Now, *here's* my first-semester report card as a freshman."

Math, history, English, Latin, Sociology—everything. Straight A's. A 4.0. "It's perfect," I droned.

"And it's remained perfect since then," she said. "At the end of this school year, I'll graduate with a 4.0, with a dual degree in Physics and Chemistry, and I've got an honors scholarship for my post-grad work. Yale."

I didn't know what to say or even think.

Going Monstering

She put the book back and took me to the candle-lit desk. I could see the outline of her perfect body through the sheer nightie. "My point, Ann, is that if I can do it, you most certainly can. You have the power to be all that I am, and more." She smiled. "It's not easy for me to admit that you have much more potential, much more sheer *promise*, than I did when I started Pledge Week."

Potential? Promise? She was saying this about *me*.

Me...

"So don't worry." She kissed me lightly on the cheek. "Just do your best tomorrow, then on Saturday you'll be inducted as an official Sister of Alpha House. Everything will be fine." She sat back down.

I felt so much better now. My own parents never had faith in me, but Kezzy *did*. I was about to say something else but then I saw that she was reading that book again...

"Miss Kezzy? What's that book you're reading?"

Her face glowed in the candlelight. "*This* book you can think of as a catalog of translations, Ann. The translations—or I should say tran*scriptions*—were written in the late-1600's, by a man named Joseph Corwan—"

"The man in the portrait downstairs."

"Exactly."

"I found it kind of odd, Miss Kezzy, I mean, how similar the names are."

"The names?"

"Well, Joseph Corwan, and then the college founder, Joseph Curwen. Were they related in some way?"

She paused for some reason. "Yes, but only distantly. You see, Corwan's transcriptions are important; it's not this book, so much, Ann," and she patted the book in front of her, "but the original book from which these transcriptions were made. Would you like to hear about it?"

"Sure, Miss Kezzy."

She leaned back in the old, high chair, and crossed her legs under herself. "A long time ago, a poet from the Middle East named Abdul Alhazred wrote a book in Syria. You can think of Alhazred as sort of a motivational philosopher, for in a sense, his book was one of motivational and philosophical science. The name of that book was *Al Azif*."

Right away, I remembered. "That's the word written under the Alpha House 'A.'"

"You're very observant, Ann, yes. Now, the original copy of Al Azif no longer exists but over the centuries it was translated, first, into Greek, then Latin, German, Spanish, and even English. These later translations were retitled The Necronomicon. But there was a problem, for some of these translations were flawed."

"You mean somebody fucked 'em up?" I asked.

Kezzy sighed. "Yes, Ann, somebody *fucked* some of them *up*, most probably on purpose."

"But why?"

"During the transcription process, detractors of the book would *deliberately* misquote it, to reduce its power as a...motivational tool."

I didn't know why she paused then, but it was still interesting. This explained why Corwan's portrait was on the wall, er — at least, sort of. "So Joseph Corwan somehow made translations that *weren't* fucked up?"

"Yes, and he's the only one in history to have been able to do that," she said. "You see, Ann, we regard *Al Azif* as the Alpha House field guide. All our sisters read the accurate translations once they're inducted." Her eyes glittered at me. "You will get to read it too. It will help you, like it helped me, and every other girl to ever be initiated into Alpha House."

This was starting to sound like some of that crackpot pseudo-science stuff but then I thought to myself, *What do I care?* I didn't care about *anything* except getting into Alpha House. One thing did cross my mind though...

"I look forward to reading it, Miss Kezzy. But one thing I

don't get is...if all the translations of the book were fucked with, how did Joseph Corwan, well...*un*fuck them?"

She paused again, in that weird way. "He was a scholar with very few peers, a language *expert*."

"Oh." Why did I feel weird now? "I'll go now, Miss Kezzy. Thanks for talking to me; it made me feel a lot better. Good-night," but when I started to move away, she grabbed my arm.

Now she whispered, grinning right at me. "I'm glad I made you feel better, Ann. Not only is that what Senior Sorority Sisters are for, it's what *friends* are for. But you know what I'd like now?"

"What, Miss Kezzy?" My shoulders slumped. "Please don't make me suck my father's dick again."

"Oh, you morbid thing, you!" she laughed but then her look turned real serious, like even maybe *desperate*. "I need you to make *me* feel better now..."

Fuck. She was making a *pass* at me? I mean, I know I'd dreamed of eating her out but I figured that was just some perverted lesbo-fantasy thing that was stowed way back in my subconscious.

Just dreams.

But *now*? Now she was putting the make on me for *real*?

"Please, Ann—oh, shit, please," and then she made me get on my knees and move under the desk. She wasn't modest— she pulled her nightie off, put her bare feet up on the chair arms, and next thing I know that perfect, hairless pussy of hers was right in my face. She pressed the back of my head. "*Please...* I just...have such a *weakness* for oral prowess..."

Oral prowess, huh? I guess that was the fancy way of her saying, *Eat my pussy*. Of course, I'd eat my own poop if she told me to—anything—but this was fucked up. Why would a super-hot-looking girl like her want *me* to do it?

I just started licking up and down, and she started hissing and flinching right off the bat. It was just like in the dream, it was *fun*. When I traded off between licking and sucking, that really got her hot. Her hands opened and closed in my hair. I could even see her pussy kind of pulsing in and out.

"Darling, darling," she whispered. "You always do it so well..."

She was getting all musky and slick, and I was really getting into it but then — *wham!* — it hit me. What she'd just said...

I *always* do it so well?

That means I'd done it *before!*

I pulled back. "Wait a minute! I've never gone down on you before! The only time I've ever done that is in my dreams!"

She looked terrified down between her legs. "Ann! Have some courtesy! You don't just *stop!*"

"So they *weren't* dreams, were they? Since the first night I got here, you really *have* been coming into my room and sitting on my face! Haven't you?"

She was all in a tizzy now. "Oh, for goodness sake — yes, Ann! So what? Seriously, what's the big deal? It's part of initiation — now, keep doing it!" and she pulled my face right back to her cookie.

How do you like that? I thought, licking away again, but then I licked a little more and — wham! — it hit me again.

I pulled back. "And if *that* wasn't really a dream, then neither was the spunk-fest at the gazebo the other night! Zenas really *did* come in my face four times, *didn't* he?"

She groaned. "All right — yes! He did! So what?" She pulled my face right back. "Now keep eating me! You're driving me nuts with this stop and start shit!"

A couple more licks, then — wham!

"Why was he talking funny for a while?" I demanded.

"Talking f — Who —"

"Zenas! The first couple times he shot his load in my face, he was talking weird, but then he started talking normal! What was that all about?"

"Oh, Ann, I have no idea what you mean —"

Wham! "And why didn't I have dried cum all over me the next morning?"

Going Monstering

She rolled her eyes, gritting her teeth. "He washed your face, then he washed and dried your nightgown, and put you to bed! Now *stop* this!" and now she grabbed my hair, twisted till it hurt, and pushed my mouth back on her. But I wrenched myself back.

"Is there a fuckin' ghost in this house?"

She looked at me like I didn't have a head.

"Seriously!" I yelled. "The stuff with you was real, and so was the stuff with Zenas at the gazebo, so maybe *that* was real, too..."

"What on *earth* are you—"

"Every night," I told her, "before you'd come in and make me eat you out, *Joseph Corwan* would come into my room—"

"Ann! He's been dead for centuries!"

"His *ghost*, I mean. He'd kind of fuck with me, and diddle with me, but I wouldn't be able to feel anything. Maybe it *was* his ghost."

CRACK!

She slapped me real hard across the face. "There's no such things as ghosts!" she growled. "You dreamed it!" She twisted my hair till I yelped. "Stop being asinine and stop this *fucking* around. You're going to eat my pussy and get me off, or I will kick you out of Alpha House and you can fly back home with your parents in the morning!"

My mouth went back to her snatch so fast I swear there was a noise like a Road Runner cartoon.

"Good, good," she murmured. "Yes, yes—oh, Ann, you do it the *best*..."

Then: another *wham!*

"The snake!" I almost shrieked.

"*What?*"

"Every night so far when I was going down on you...a *snake* shot out of your pussy and went down my throat!"

I could hear her teeth grind she was so mad now. She twisted my ear till it hurt. "You're starting to sound like a nitwit,

Edward Lee

Ann, and Alpha House has no room for *nitwits!*" She opened her pussy lips with her fingers. "Look in there. Any snakes? *Hmmm?*"

"Well...no..."

She snatched my hand and made me put two fingers in. "Feel around and tell me if there are any *snakes!*"

"No, Miss Kezzy, but—"

"No, Miss Kezzy, no Miss Kezzy—jeez!" From a desk drawer she got a little bottle of something called Astro-Glide, and squirted it all over my hand. It was real silky and slippery. "Put your whole hand in," she ordered.

"Whuh—"

She twisted my ear again till I squealed. "Put it *in!*"

"You, you want me to *fist* you?" I whined. "Oh, I don't know, Miss Kezzy. I've never done kinky stuff like that."

She stared at me, gaping. "Ann. Did you hear what you just said?"

I looked back at her, then got what she meant. "Wow. Kind of a dumb thing for me to say, huh? I mean, I've blown a dog, a chimp, and my *father*, sucked off over a hundred guys, chugged cum, licked dirty butts and drank jizz in a cup of coffee. Compared to all that, I guess fisting is pretty low on the Richter scale of kinky stuff..."

"I should say so," and then she squeezed all my fingers together and pushed them into her. "Go on, now, just push your hand the rest of the way in. Don't be timid."

I pushed, kind of wincing, then—schluck!—my hand was in to the wrist.

"Ooooo." She hissed. "Now...when I count to three, make a fist," and when she got to three I did, and she flinched, and her ass came off the chair. "Yes! Yes! Oh, honey, that's it!" She began to pant. "Now-now—please!—turn your first clockwise, then counter clockwise while moving your hand very gently back and forth..."

It was *real* tight, and I don't know how it didn't hurt.

127

Going Monstering

"More, more," she panted. "A little tiny bit harder—oh, and-and, Ann!" She touched her clit with her fingertip. "Lick right here, right here while you're doing it!"

Well, I did, and by now her clit was, like, the size of an acorn she was so turned on. Between my hand in her and my tongue there, it only took another minute, then she got all tensed up, her back arched, and her head bent back over the back of the chair, then her pussy went into a throbbing fit and began to flood around my hand. Damn, she shrieked so loud when she came, you'd think someone fuckin' stabbed her.

She wound down in another minute, grinning at me between her legs like a fat cat. Then her vagina muscles got real tight and popped my hand out.

She sighed with her head still bent back over the chair. "Did you feel any snake up there, Ann?"

"No, Miss Kezzy. I guess it was a dream, and so was the ghost..."

She smoothed her hands over her boobs and down her belly, still sighing. "Oh, Ann, that was so good," and then, then...

She moaned something to herself that sounded like, "Neb g'nurgln, eb shub soom'x, *eeeeeeeeeeee*-ahhhhhhhh..."

I stared right at her. "Those words... They sound just like..."

She ran her fingers through my hair. "Like what, Ann? Similar to words you've heard before? Hmmm?"

"Yeah." I gulped. "Every night, in the middle of the night, real low. But I thought, I thought...it was a dream too."

"It wasn't, Ann. It's a tape loop that plays automatically at certain times of the night. It's *subliminal*. The words sink into your subconscious mind." She stroked my cheek. "They're words from *Al Azif*." She finally sat back up in the chair and took a deep breath. "Well, that was very nice, Ann—thank you, but you'd best run along now and get to bed. You'll need your rest."

I started to leave but turned around at the door. "Miss Kezzy? I want to know what those words mean."

She wasn't looking at me when she answered. She was looking back at the book. "You'll find out tomorrow night."

☠ ☠ ☠

THE next morning was kind of hilarious. My parents and Hannah's parents were all so embarrassed, their faces were pink at breakfast. They apologized over and over to Kezzy for getting so drunk last night. "I'm so ashamed!" my mother said. "I hope I didn't do anything silly!" "There's no excuse for me to have had so many wines," dad said to Kezzy. "I truly apologize," then he scribbled out a check, "but I hope this donation to Alpha House will, if only slightly, improve your opinion of us." Hannah's father wrote out a check, too. "Please don't hold our irresponsibility against our daughters, Kezzy."

Kezzy took the checks without even looking at them. "That could never happen, sir, and don't be too hard on yourselves for having a good time." Kezzy winked at me. "We all get a little wild on occasion."

When Zenas was getting the Rolls, my father pulled me aside into the living room.

"Ann. I don't know what to say about my behavior last night." He squinted at me. "Did I get all...pissy-drunk?"

"Well, you and mom definitely threw a few back, but don't worry about it."

He stood there shifting his feet, like he was uncomfortable. "I'm...sorry for the way I've treated you all these years. Sometimes the truth takes a while to hit home."

"What do you mean, dad?"

"Before breakfast, Kezzy told me that you were the finest pledge she'd ever encountered, that you've worked harder than

Going Monstering

any of them. That really made be pause to wonder." Now he was wringing his hands. "It doesn't matter that you've had problems growing up; what *does* matter is that, regardless, a girl needs a father who's encouraging, supportive, understanding, not just a big stick. I've been terribly derogatory, Ann—not a father at all but a perfect asshole. But what I want you to know... is that I'm proud of you."

I actually gulped.

"I've never said that before, have I?"

All I could do was shake my head.

"Forgive me, Ann," and then—oh, fuck!—the piece of shit was wiping tears from his eyes!

"It's all right, dad," I said.

"When will you know if you're in?"

"Tomorrow."

"Kezzy told me that after all your hard work thus far, you're *guaranteed* to be admitted. I couldn't be happier for you. But, tell me, what sorts of things have you had to do in the way of pledge initiations?"

Dad, if you only knew. "Mostly just studying," I lied.

He looked so proud of me just then. He didn't look like himself at all. "I look forward to hearing from you tomorrow, Ann. Your mother and I love you very much..."

What an uncomfortable scene. When the rest of the mushy goodbyes were done, Zenas drove them back to the airport.

It was really cool that Kezzy had told him all those great things about me, especially the part of about me being guaranteed to make it into Alpha House. There was only one more hazing left, and I wasn't even worried about it.

But, you know? I was worried about something.

Kezzy gave us the afternoon off, told us we could do anything we wanted. We weren't leaving till five. After a fuckin' unflavored-yogurt lunch, I went outside 'cos Hannah said she'd meet me there in a while. It was a beautiful day, sun shining, warm, birds chirping. The fountains were gushing. I sat at the gazebo just to kind of clear my head. The way I was sitting, I had my back to the house.

"Hi, Ann," an upbeat girl's voice said behind me, but when I started to turn to see who it was, she said, "Don't turn around! You can't see me — otherwise, this won't work..."

I froze in the chair. My stomach started knotting up.

"You recognize my voice, don't you?"

I sure did. "Mmmm...*Mercy.*"

"Yeah. It's good to see you, Ann."

Birds chirped through a long pause. "We, uh, we heard you were dead. It was on the news," I whispered.

"Oh, yeah. I *am* dead. The night I left, I got killed when the cab crashed. None of that matters, though."

I gulped. It sounded like she really was right behind me. "How can getting killed not matter?"

Birds kept chirping. "When I died, I went to Heaven, Ann. That's all that matters. *God's* all that matters."

I was scared shitless. Was there really a *dead person* standing behind me?

"You could go to Heaven someday, too, Ann...but not if you join Alpha House."

Part of me really wanted to turn around, to prove to myself that I was either hearing things or Kezzy was there somehow imitating Mercy's voice. But then another part of me was too scared, because what if I really *did* see Mercy?

The gazebo was made of all dark-stained wood that had been varnished and was real shiny. In one of the wooden rails in front of me, I could see, or *thought* I could see, a reflection of a person. It was warped and went off to one side like one of those mirrors at a carnival, but the reflection was thin, kind of flesh-colored, and human-shaped. It looked like a nude girl...

"Mercy...are you...naked?"

"Of course! There are no clothes in Heaven because there's no lust and no shame. All we wear is the natural beauty that God gave us."

Going Monstering

I squinted at the reflection. Yes, a skinny girl with dark hair and...

There was a big dark clump between the girl's legs, like a huge amount of pubic hair. *I guess they don't have Lady Remingtons in Heaven.* "Are you really here, Mercy, or am I imagining this?"

"Oh, I'm really here, Ann, but I can't stay long." It was the same high-pitched, bubbly voice she always had. "I came here to tell you something. I came here to tell you that Alpha House is evil. It's an insult to God. He even told me that himself. He said that Alpha House is an *umbrage.*"

"*He?* You mean *God* told you that?"

"Yes! I talked to him today. He's great. But you'll never get to meet Him unless you leave. Ann, so far you've passed every initiation by the power of your own free will. Now you have to use that same free will to walk out. Will you do that?"

I stared at the reflection. "I...I don't think so..."

The reflection moved, got closer, and then I felt a hand touch my shoulder. "Leave Alpha House. Take Hannah and leave Alpha House before tonight..."

I turned around and, of course, no one was there.

Fuck, I thought. I didn't need this headache. Was I cracking up? Next thing I knew, Hannah was coming across the backyard. She sat down across from me in the gazebo. "Ann. You look like you've been doing 'shrooms or acid or something."

I was still staring so I snapped myself out of it. "I sort of feel like that, like a bad trip all of a sudden."

Hannah clasped her hands together, looking concerned. "You're worried, I know, just like me. We're so close..."

Yeah. But now I was wondering exactly what we were getting so close to. I didn't say anything about Mercy—shit, what *could* I say? I was pretty sure I didn't believe it. And last night? *Oh, Hannah, last night when I was FISTING Kezzy, she said some really weird stuff that's been making me wonder?* No, I couldn't say that. All I said was this: "Hannah, I've been thinking."

"Me, too. Like, what will we have to do for our last initiation?"

It was on my mind, sure, but *that's* not what bothered me most. "Hannah, do you hear...weird words at night sometimes? Like, when you're asleep and you might wake up for a second?"

She shook her head. "No, but I've always been a heavy sleeper."

I couldn't press it if she hadn't heard it herself; it would just make me sound nuttier. But now it struck me that those weird words on the tape loop Kezzy admitted to playing sounded... well, they sounded kind of *satanic. That's* what I'd been thinking. Like maybe that's what Alpha House was really all about, some sort of witch-coven or satanic cult. First, there was Kezzy pitching a fit over Mercy's cross, and then the whole *virgin* thing. Maybe Corwan or Curwen or even both of them had hidden a devil-worshiping cult in the sorority, that they'd deliberately made it a rule that only virgins could get in. I didn't believe in shit like that but—fuck—what was I supposed to think? Maybe the words on the tape loop were some sort of spell or incantation, and that book of translations Kezzy was reading out of all the time.... Maybe it was some kind of satanic bible.

Maybe we were being set up.

Hannah looked fretful. "What do *you* think the final initiation will be?"

My voice sounded like sandpaper. "I think we'll be losing our virginity," I said, but then I thought, *Either that, or Kezzy's gonna sacrifice us...*

💀 💀 💀

Going Monstering

WE left in the Rolls about 7 p.m. Wasn't a lot of talking at first. Kezzy fussed with her hair and lipstick while me and Hannah sat holding hands in the back seat, kind of shaking like we had a chill, only it was eighty degrees. After an hour on the road, I asked, "Miss Kezzy? Where are we going tonight?"

"A little north of Providence. It should take about two more hours to get there." She looked back and grinned. "We're going to a farm."

Hannah's jaw locked open, but I groaned, "I should've known. Farm animals..."

Kezzy laughed. "I thought that would get some life out of you. But, no, girls, you won't be required to engage in any sexual contact with farm animals—"

"Thank God!" Hannah exclaimed.

"You see, *this* farm has been abandoned for decades. There're no cows or pigs or chickens anymore. In fact, the original farmhouse is no longer standing. It burned down in 1771."

"Then...why are we going there?" I asked.

"It's of historical significance—the *property*, I should say. It was once owned by a very successful merchant named Joseph Curwen—who, incidentally, died the same night the farmhouse burned down. You girls already *know* who that is, don't you—*Hannah?*"

Kezzy knew *I* knew. She glared at Hannah, who stammered a minute, then said, "Oh, yeah! He's the guy who founded the college."

"Good. Since Pledge Week is winding down now, and since I have every confidence that both of you ladies will be inducted into Alpha House tomorrow, I think that now is the time for me to be a bit more *forthright* with critical information. You may find it difficult to believe or you may not but either way it scarcely matters." She got something out of her purse. "Ann, you're clearly the more *observant* pledge. Let me show you something. Look at it, then tell me what you think," and then she handed me her key-ring, and said, "Examine that, please."

"Just a bunch of fuckin' keys, Miss Kezzy," I said.

Her voice rose. "Well then *fuckin'* examine it with more scrutiny."

Then I saw what she meant. One of the things on the ring wasn't a key. It was a rectangular piece of metal about two inches long. It looked old. "This thing here...it looks like..."

It was a brass nameplate, dark from tarnish. It had a screwhole in either end, and it was through one of those holes that the ring itself passed. I squinted at the barely readable engraving.

Joseph Corwan, Esquire & Gentleman
of the Colony of Rhode Island.
b. February 28, 1662
d. April 12, 1771

"Well, Ann?"

I didn't catch it at first. "This is just like the nameplate under the portrait in the living room only it's the original one, isn't it? This one's real old but the one there now looks new."

"That's because it *is* new. But surely that's not *all* you find noteworthy about the plate."

The dates, I noticed. "Wait a minute..." *Born in 1662 and died in 1771!* "The dates are fucked up, Miss Kezzy! According to *this* plate, Corwan lived to be..." Five minutes later, I figured, "A hundred and nine years old!"

"Mind like a steel trap."

"But that's impossible, Miss Kezzy," Hannah said. "No one lives that long."

"Actually, a handful of people *have* lived that long, but it's

Going Monstering

very, very rare," Kezzy said.

I was already smelling something fishy. "Somebody changed the dates. This plate was replaced with the new one, and the new one says that Corwan died in 1711."

"Precisely. And can you surmise why?"

My head was ticking. "Curwen and Corwan are two differ-ent people, you said so last night, said that they were distantly related. And a minute ago you said that Curwen, not Corwan, died in 1771. So..." I stared at her. "You lied?"

"I obfuscated the truth," Kezzy said, still fussing in the visor mirror, "for a number of reasons, the most paramount of which is discreetness. An epitaph claiming that a man lived 109 years might raise some brows, so that's why the phony plate was put in its stead. And, yes, I lied about Corwan's relationship to Cur-wen. They were actually both the same man."

The car's tires hummed over the road. The sun was setting.

"In 1692, Corwan moved from Salem to Providence, and he did so with some haste," Kezzy went on. "You see, he was a warlock."

Me and Hannah huddled closer.

"A few too many indiscretions promulgated his exit from Salem, after which he immediately changed his name to get shed of his previous reputation. Joseph Corwan became Joseph Curwen once he was settled in the Stamper's Hill area of Provi-dence. And there he lived for decades in relative anonymity."

"But you said he was a warlock," I said. "That's, like, a dev-il-worshiper, right?"

"Yes, it is, or at least that's what the peasant sensibilities of the day ascertained. In truth, though, it was not the devil that Joseph Curwen lived to serve for multiple decades. It was in-stead something far worse than devils, and Curwen was able to perpetuate his blasphemous reverence only by an inexhaustible knowledge of Abdul Alhazred..."

"The guy who wrote that book," I remembered. "*Al Azif.* You were reading the translations last night."

"Yes, Ann. You and Hannah will too eventually. Once you have received the proper predilections to understand it. Joseph Curwen was one of history's most significant sorcerers. From *Al Azif* he learned, among other things, the secret of transferring his consciousness into the bodies of others, mostly kin, which is how he was able to walk the earth for so long. Another secret he learned was that of 'Rendering of Essential Saltes,' quite a fascinating feat. He spent decades enlisting the services of graverobbers, who would pilfer the bones of some of the world's greatest thinkers *and* warlocks. Utilizing the proper spells and laboratory treatments, Curwen was able to reduce the bones down to their essential salts, and with those salts he learned perhaps a great secret indeed, 'The Secret of Raising Shades.'"

"Raising—" Hannah began.

"Shades?" I finished.

"Shades as opposed to blinds?" Hannah asked.

Kezzy shook her head. "You'll understand in due time." She rolled down the window and smiled up at the moon. "For the next hour or so, let's be still in our own thoughts and contemplate the enormity of our blessings. You see, girls, tonight... we're going Monstering..."

SO that was the light at the end of the Alpha House rainbow. First Old Manning, then Bumming, Kenneling, Rednecking, Chimping, Fathering, and now...*now*... *Monstering.*

I'd been right about the truth behind Alpha House. It was an occult sorority, a coven or something. But did I believe it?

I didn't know—that's the funny thing. Any other time, of *course* I wouldn't believe it, but now...there was something in the air, a *vibe*, I don't know. I was prepared to believe anything.

After a while, Kezzy explained the rest. Curwen paid guys to dig up the bones of other sorcerers, and then did stuff to the bones to get these "essential salts," and then with these salts he could bring back the dead. He'd bring these dead warlocks back to life and then torture them for information, for their secrets. I don't know what the process was, just doing egghead stuff in a laboratory and reading special spells from the book. Human sacrifice had plenty to do with it too but somehow I knew that Kezzy wasn't going to sacrifice me and Hannah. I could feel that in my heart, I *knew* it when I looked up at the stars.

But the thing holding Curwen back had been the book itself, this *Necronomicon*, which was originally the book that guy Alhazred wrote, *Al Azif*. A lot of the translations were fucked up on purpose by the people who transcribed the original copies. Curwen had to find a way of getting the *real* translations of the most important parts of the book.

He raised the "Shade" of Abdul Alhazred.

See, Alhazred was supposedly eaten alive in broad daylight by an invisible demon he accidentally called up with the jive in the book. Most of his body disappeared right in front of everybody while the demon swallowed it but, see, you know how when you eat a piece of fried chicken, some little crumbs fall on the floor? That's kind of what happened, only the "crumb" was Alhazred's hand. Then some guy on the street picked the hand up and ran off with it, and from that time on, the bones of the hand were sold back and forth from one collector to another. Eventually, like, a *thousand years* after Alhazred was killed, Curwen managed to buy those bones from some guy in Europe. Then he brought Alhazred back to life and tortured him until he agreed to translate the critical passages correctly. And once Curwen got all the info he needed, he dissolved Alhazred's Shade in acid.

There were a lot of secrets in Al Azif, but the biggest one wasn't how to raise Shades or keep your spirit alive in other people's bodies. What Curwen ultimately learned from Al-hazred was how to "Solicit the Gate by Where the Spheres Do Meet." See, it wasn't the *devil* that Curwen worshiped, it wasn't *demons*. It was a bunch of these fucked up things from another dimension with names like Yog-Sothoth and Nyarlathotep and Azathoth and Cthulhu. Anybody who learned *Al Azif's* secrets as good as Curwen did, they could actually go to this other dimension, they could *see* the cities there, and sometimes they could even...

Bring things from there to here.

There was a long line of people who followed in Curwen's footsteps but they weren't warlocks, they were *sorceresses*, and they still exist to this day. Can you guess where they operate from?

That's right. Alpha House.

After about three hours on the road, we were really deep in the boonies. Scrubland, hills, and more scrubland. Earlier a sign said Pawtucket Road, and I think we stayed on that a long time. This must be the farmland Curwen owned so long ago, and when we saw this old foundation sitting up on one of the low hills, Kezzy told us that's where Curwen's original farm-house had been before it got burned down by a bunch of pissed off locals. The farmhouse was just a disguise; it was really his laboratory and temple, where he did all his experiments and rituals. There'd even been a passage under the house that led to this whole network of tunnels and rooms underground but the villagers blew it up, thinking that no one would ever be able to find them again. They were wrong about that.

It was past ten o'clock when Zenas turned the Rolls down this dirt road that went through the woods. Then he stopped.

"Heer we is, folks."

Fuck, I thought.

"Wait," Hannah said, "we've seen that before, haven't we?"

"Is the dim bulb burning a bit brighter these days?" Kezzy sniggered.

"It's that shack from the painting in Kezzy's room," I said.

Kezzy's—correction, *fuckin'* Kezzy's eyes widened. "*Pardon me, Ann?*"

"I mean, *Miss* Kezzy's room," I said. *Barbie doll battle-ax....*

That's what we were looking at, that shitty little wood-plank shack, the same as the one in the painting. The only difference was the windows were boarded up now, and the place was crawling with ivy and was half-swallowed by the trees all around it. "But in the fuckin' painting there aren't many trees. It's just sort of sitting in the middle of all this fucked-up shitty-looking land," I said.

"Your powers of observation just keeping getting more and more refined, Ann, along with you language. But it's because the painting was rendered in the mid-1700's; since then many trees have reared up in the 'shitty-looking' land. *All* of this land was once the Curwen estate, and it still is in a sense. His endowment was quite large and was left to Alpha House. We pay the taxes. We ensure that this land is never sold to a developer. And this bungalow? It was once an ancillary building for the farm workers' quarters. It's importance is immeasurable, because, like the farmhouse, it contains an access to the tunnel-network underground."

"And we're going there," I said more than asked. "Now."

Kezzy grinned in the moonlight. "Yes. We are."

Hannah grabbed me, shivering. "So what's, what's...Monstering?"

"We're gonna have to fuck a monster..."

Kezzy just kept grinning.

We all got out, and Zenas—still in his maid's suit, by the way—got a bunch of stuff out of the trunk. But Kezzy just stood there looking at the shack in some kind of quiet joy. The moon glowed down, and all around us we could hear crickets peeping. After giving us each a lantern, Zenas unlocked the front door and led the way with a real bright flashlight. He had a knapsack on, and I could see that corner of the big book of transcriptions sticking out.

141

Going Monstering

The shack was empty inside. There were inches of dust on the floor but you could see a trail of footprints in it. It was obvious that year after year, for all this time, the pledges were brought to this place. In a back room, I saw some old wash tubs, and a platform. Zenas fiddled with something, and then the platform slid to the side. In the space beneath was an open manhole. A draft gusted up, and we all almost gagged.

"Don't mind the smell, ladies," Kezzy said. "It will abate in short order."

Fuck, I thought. It stunk.

"Yawl ready?" Zenas drawled.

Kezzy nodded, then leveled her gaze on me and Hannah. "Consider yourselves possessed of an utmost privilege. *Very few people* have ever made the journey you are about to..."

Hannah kept shivering, but for some reason I wasn't scared at all, not even when we all climbed down an iron ladder through this cement tube straight down until we came to some brick steps which led down even further.

It really did stink—like rotten stuff, meat and vegetables, maybe, all mixed with the smell of wet dirt. But Kezzy was right; the stink didn't last. Now the draft seemed to flow against our backs, like somewhere else there might be a vent drawing the old air out. The more we walked, the older the passage seemed to get, and the more narrow. I could see by my lantern that the walls were really old brick covered with this gross fungus or moss. There were dripping sounds, and the floor felt slimy beneath my sneakers.

"Yuck," Hannah kept saying. "Yuck, yuck, yuck!"

"Oh, don't be such a milquetoast," Kezzy said.

Then came more steps that went down in three slants. Our footsteps echoed and our lights bobbed. Eventually we came to a big brick-walled room that was lined with stone archways that when you held your lantern up in them, all you could see was blackness that seemed to go on forever. But some of the archways had old wooden doors that had been touched up or repaired over the years.

"How, how deep are we under the ground, Miss Kezzy?" Hannah stammered.

"You don't want to know..."

But I asked, "What's behind these doors, Miss Kezzy?"

"Storage rooms, ante-rooms, several of Joseph Curwen's initial laboratories, and the like."

An abrupt spattering sound rose, and Hannah screamed.

"Aw, naow, durn't get'cher dander up," Zenas said, his back to us. He had that hog of a cock out and was pissing on a wall. "Just tekin' myself a pee."

"You're so genteel," Kezzy frowned in the lantern light. "What do they do without you at Harvard Yard."

"Hah-vud...*huh?*"

"Just shut up and finish pissing, you inarticulate *manimal.*" Kezzy pointed to one of the doors. "Ann, look in that room there, and show Hannah."

The old door clicked open and we stuck our heads into a very musty blackness. I raised my lantern —

Hannah screamed again, this time so loud I swear her hair stood on end. *Fuck!* I thought. The brick-walled room contained a pile of skeletons so high it almost went to the ceiling.

Kezzy was laughing when Hannah finally stopped screaming. "Blood is as essential to a warlock as bricks are to a mason. Curwen sacrificed many dupes for their blood and other attributes when his experiments called for it. Mostly illegal immigrants who took jobs on his ships. Among other things, Curwen owned a very successful shipping business. He also used the burliest of these men to subdue the Shades once they were resurrected."

So far, I think Hannah had just let all the Curwen/warlock stuff go in one ear and out the other, but now her eyes looked a little zapped after seeing that room full of skeletons. There must've been a hundred of them in there.

Another door took us through the most normal-looking

room yet, like a study or an office, with a desk, a table, book-shelves and old furniture. A bunch of old oil lamps sat on the floor, and on the wall hung a chart with a human body on it showing all the muscles and veins and stuff. There was another chart full of squares, with letters in each square, like H, and He, and Pb, and Ca. I think I remembered it from a high school chemistry class, which the only reason I passed was because I blew the teacher a couple times. But the bookshelves here were all empty and full of cobwebs.

"The contents of Joseph Curwen's entire occult library have been removed, for safe-keeping, to —"

"The *Alpha House* library," I said.

"Correct, Ann. Along with many other invaluable oddments, documents, and correspondence." She grinned at us again, but it was more like grinning to herself in some private glee. "All of his secrets have been passed on to us." Her eyes flashed. "*All* of them. We are the Keepers of those secrets, the Custodians."

"Oh, you mean like a janitor," Hannah said. "So I guess you keep all the books clean, huh, Miss Kezzy?"

Kezzy glared. "Hannah, it's your very good fortune that the phenomenally *anserine* are allowed to live."

"Anser..."

"Just be quiet, Hannah," I said and elbowed her, but I didn't know what the word meant either.

After that, Kezzy took us down another passage but stopped. She faced us and put on one of those surgical mask thingies like you see doctors wear on TV show. Then she handed one to me, Hannah, and Zenas. "Don these," she said.

Hannah squinted. "Who's...*Don?*"

Kezzy put her fingers through her hair. "Hannah. If you had your brain removed and replaced with Spam, you'd likely be smarter."

"*Spam? Ooo, yuck!* I hate that stuff!"

"'Don we now our gay apparel?'" I said and pinched her. "Put the mask on! I think where she's taking us next will stink!"

"Oh..."

We put them on, then...

Kezzy opened another door in one of the archways.

We walked into this big room full of pillars that had a stone slab in the middle. Nobody needed to be told what this place was. Dozens of people, I told myself, no, HUNDREDS—*butchered in here*... More archways lined the place, and some had cage-doors but I didn't see anything behind them,

The mask worked a little but I could still smell something *awful*. I just forced myself to hack it and got diverted when I roved my lantern around while looking down at the floor. There were these irregular slabs, maybe slate, laying around in different areas. They had holes drilled in them. Immediately I thought, *Airholes*...

Kezzy said, "It's normally cacophonic in here—"

"Caco—*what*?" Hannah whined. "Miss Kezzy, do you mean we have to suck more cocks?"

Kezzy looked fit to scream. "Zenas, if she says *one more stupid thing*...I want you to sodomize her with such *vigor* that her asshole turns inside-out."

"Wal, naow, thet wurn't be no problem at all."

I grabbed Hannah tight by the collar. "Just *shut up*..."

"When I say cacophonic I mean *noisy*," Kezzy said through her mask. "We quell such bothersome noise—known as The Cauterwauling—with a Spell of Muteness. I will remove that spell for a moment, just so you girls get the idea. Prepare yourselves," and then Kezzy yelled, "In nomen of Yog-Sothoth , ego levo vestri mutus!" and in that split second, me and Hannah fell to our knees screaming. Suddenly the stone room was full of a sound like a waterfall in hell. Things were howling, moaning, wailing. High-pitched and low-pitched mewls that couldn't be human and couldn't be from any animal I'd ever heard of. Even when we covered our ears, that barely cut the sound. I was crying it was so awful, but when I looked up at Kezzy and Zenas, they were both smiling at us.

145

Going Monstering

"Make it STOP!" I begged.

Her brows shot up like she was offended. *"Pardon me, Ann?"*

OH, FOR FUCK'S SAKE! "Make it stop, *Miss Kezzy,* PLEASE!"

She tapped her foot for a minute, then said, "In nomen of Yog Sothoth, may totus exsisto silens!"

The waterfall howling stopped.

Hannah and me convulsed on the slimy floor for awhile, but finally my ears stopped ringing and I got my head back together. "Miss Kezzy. The things making that noise...they're under those slabs, aren't they?"

"Yes, Ann. Some are Shades of Joseph Curwen's enemies, or current raisings of brilliant men whose interrogation had not been completed upon Curwen's death. Typically, Curwen would put down a Shade after raising it; hence, reverting it back to its original essential salts for future use. Others he would raise simply for the pleasure of torture, after which he would destroy them forever with corrosives. That's what he did with the Shade of Abdul Alhazred, for he didn't want to risk the chance of some other warlock stealing the poet's salts for his own gleaning. There are also some mistakes here, which Curwen never put down simply because he enjoyed the grotesqueness of their imperfect condition."

"Mistakes?" I asked.

"On rare occasions the essential salts of a procurement would be *imperfect*, or tainted by an overlooked — or deliberate — contaminant. The Shade might then be raised, for instance, without limbs, or with *switched* limbs, or externalized organs, or any other manner of defect." Kezzy pointed to one of the slabs. "That one there, Zenas."

"Shuh thing..." Zenas stuck his fingers in two of the holes in a slab, and lifted it off like it was styrofoam.

"Bring your lanterns, girls, and look in..."

We took our time doing it 'cos neither of us wanted to see what was in the hole. I finally got my courage up and did it first, leaning over, then taking a breath, and looking down.

At first I didn't see anything, just a circular cement pit twenty feet deep. The sides of the pit were slimy with moss or mold. "There's nothing...," but then I squinted and *did* see something, sitting at the very bottom.

"This is the Shade of the Honorable Goodman Briden," Kezzy said, "a notably zealous judge in the Salem Courts of the late-1600's. Briden was the first to be suspicious of Joseph *Corwan's* character, which then forced Corwan to flee the town and change his name. Curwen deliberately tainted the judge's salts in order to cause his Shade to be raised *vacuus tergum*, meaning skinless."

I made out a form which I then recognized as the top of a man's head. I thought I heard a slapping sound. Then the head moved, and a face looked up.

A *skinless* face.

The face was red and veiny; you could see all the muscles, and the big white lidless eyes. I almost hurled.

A wet slapping noise fluttered up. *What is he... Oh, fuck!*

He was beating off...with a skinless dick.

"After so much time, many Shades go mad, like Judge Briden here. Male Shades not put down tend to masturbate perpetually, for there's little else left to do."

Then those lidless eyes looked right at me, and he shrieked.

Zenas put the lid back on, then lifted off another.

"Girls," Kezzy said, pointing into the next pit. "Joseph Curwen paid grave-robbers a princely sum for the bones of *this* man..."

Me and Hannah looked down and saw this old balding guy with a big bushy gray beard. "Who...who is it?" Hannah asked.

"One of the wisest men to ever live," Kezzy said. "Ladies, meet Galileo. You do know who Galileo is, don't you...*Hannah?*"

Hannah looked like she was about to faint. "I, I...um—oh, shit!"

Kezzy's eyes burned like hot coals she was so mad. "You don't know who *Galileo* is? Hannah! You're a disgrace! Your ignorance is unsurpassed!" She tapped her foot.

"I think he was Italian," I blabbered.

"Oh, oh!" Hannah stammered. "Is he, like, like, the guy who invented pizza?" Kezzy glared. "Zenas. Get your cock out."

"Wal, I'd be happy tew," the meat-rack said and hauled it all out. He started flapping it up and down.

Kezzy's face came right up to me. "Ann. If you can't tell me who fucking Galileo is, Zenas will turn Hannah's asshole inside-out with his dick."

My brain started spinning. *Galileo?* I knew I'd heard of him but... He was some guy from olden times, from Italy, but that's all I knew. Hannah was blubbering while Zenas—hard already—started to pull her pants down.

"Ann! Help me!"

"He was, like—oh, he was a guy who, like, looked at shit with telescopes and shit!"

Kezzy sighed and called Zenas off. "Your answer, Ann—*feeble* though it may be—is correct. Galileo revolutionized math as a component of natural philosophy and, even more important, created astronomical tenets that verified the heliocentric system."

The only reason I passed astronomy in high school was 'cos—well, you can probably guess...

From the pit, this Galileo dude yelled, "Nel famoso di Paradiso , rilascio me!"

Kezzy grinned and waved, "Bye-bye, bye-bye," while Zenas put back the lid.

A different accent shot up from the next hole, "Vous méchant sorciⅡre! Mai une maudire Λtre sur vous!"

Kezzy giggled and said his name was Felix something, the fifth, I think. The guy had been a pope in the 1400's, or maybe she said anti-pope, whatever that means. "Zenas," she said, "give the Padre something to liven up his papal apartment," and she laughed and laughed while Zenas pulled down his pantyhose, hung his hairy ass over the hole, and started dropping foot-long turds on this guy. The guy bellowed.

In another pit was some guy with his legs where his arms should be, his arms where his legs should be, his head where his ass should be, and his ass sitting on his shoulders, and in another pit there was this pretty good-looking girl—"The comeliest of the Devonshire witches," Kezzy said—but she had no arms or legs. They hadn't been cut off, they just *weren't there*. Curwen had done something to this one's essential salts to make her that way, for "carnal fun and games," Kezzy said.

Me and Hannah were both dizzy from looking at these things, and I was glad that Kezzy didn't make us look into every pit. My stomach was squirming. "How long have these things been here, Miss Kezzy?"

"Why, for hundreds of years, of course. What you must understand is that Shades don't die since, in an obvoluted way, they're already dead. Only Alpha House sisters have been down in this holy place since Curwen's physical death. The magic of the Old Ones is why they've remained alive all this time."

Hundreds of years, I thought. *Just sitting down there, stinking, decade after decade, century after century...* "Why not just put them out of their misery?"

Kezzy walked around, her heels tapping. "While it's true that the overall majority of the Shades no longer have any use, their misery is the *point*. To put them out of their misery, Ann, would contradict the wishes of our benefactor. This will be crystal-clear to you, in time." She sat up on the stone slab in the middle of the pillars. "Curwen discovered secrets upon secrets, girls. And rest assured, he is among us now." Zenas took the *Al Azif* translations out of the knapsack, and then he flicked a cigarette lighter and lit something inside this tin ball with holes in it. The ball was on the end of a chain.

But what had she said? Curwen was among us now? "You mean Curwen's ghost?" I asked.

"His *discorporation*," she said. "The spirits of evil men are particularly potent, Ann. But, yes, you've seen Curwen a num-

Going Monstering

ber of times. He prowls Alpha House with regularity, especially in vicinity to Pledge Week."

Now Zenas was swaying the tin ball back and forth on its chain while smoke came out of the holes.

"Oh my God, oh my God, oh my God!" Hannah blabbered.

I saw it too. Behind the smoke, like something half-real, I could see Curwen standing there, in the same old-style clothes I'd seen him in those nights he came into my room.

"Through the torture of Alhazred's Shade, Curwen received the true translations of *Al Azif's* most powerful passages, and he passed all that knowledge on to us. To *Alpha House*. Ascending Nodes, Descending Nodes, Ye Casting of ye Divell's Mark, and many many more."

"That night at the gazebo," I said. "That wasn't Zenas the whole time, was it?"

"No, Ann. It was Zenas loaning Curwen the use of his body, to fully experience the delights of orgasm. Curwen's quite a randy warlock. I was able to effect this by reading the *Ritus Imitor*, which I will do again tonight." Her eyes sparkled in the lantern light. "But it won't be *Zenas's* body that Curwen's spirit will borrow."

Then I remembered what she'd said earlier.

Tonight...we're going Monstering...

Hannah clung to me, in tears. "What's she *talking* about, Ann?"

My voice was a dark croak. "She's gonna put Curwen's spirit inside a monster...then *we* get fucked by the monster..."

Kezzy just kept grinning. "Take off your clothes, ladies."

We were pretty much zombies by then. After all that had happened up to now? And after what we'd seen in those pits? We dragged our clothes off, staring at nothing.

I was afraid to ask but I asked anyway, "Where's the monster, Miss Kezzy?"

"Oh, it's here. But the more efficacious question would be... *what's* the monster?"

Edward Lee

Zenas was lifting another lid.

Just the idea of it made me and Hannah crouch back into the corner. But for some reason, Kezzy turned her head *away* from Zenas, and she was grimacing.

"Prop the lid against the wall facing away. God, how the *sight* of the Sign disgusts me so...

Sign? But then I saw that the next lid had these marking on top of it, star-shaped outlines with funny stuff written in them. I looked at it but—

"Oww!" I yelled. "That makes my head hurt!"

"It's the Elder Sign," Kezzy told us. "We had to draw one on that particular lid...to keep the cell's guest quelled. The reason that you've gotten a headache from it is due to the fact that you and Hannah both are in the infancy of your metamorphosis from regular girl...to Alpha House girl."

I didn't know what she was talking about, but the headache stopped the second Zenas turned those star-shapes away from us. I could think again, and I remembered her question. "So, Missy Kezzy...*what* is the monster?"

She didn't say anything at first, because this slopping-like noise along with a gurgling came from the open pit. It got louder and louder, until...

Something began to crawl out.

Me and Hannah screamed.

"This is not a Shade, ladies," Kezzy said. "It's a Shoggoth. It was not raised, it was *transported* to us—"

"From *where?*" I shrieked when I got my first look at it.

"From a para-planar interstice, which is easier just to think of as another dimension. It was brought here a long time ago, in the 1760's...by Joseph Curwen, who successfully utilized one of *Al Azif's* most spectacular passages."

When the thing got itself all the way out of the pit, it just sat there, kind of throbbing, and behind the stone slab near the pillars, I could still see that smoke coming out of the tin ball, and behind the smoke was the ghost of Joseph Curwen.

151

Going Monstering

The ghost smiled.

But the thing from the pit? It was just a big pile of slop. When I squinted, I could make out details 'cos there was something *about* it that made my vision shift. The only comparison I can think of is to say it looked like a pile of Super Balls — you've seen them, the kind that are clear but have sparkly stuff inside — only the balls were all held together by slime.

"A Shoggoth is an entity specifically manufactured for labor and war," Kezzy went on. "They are composed of inorganic matter — called *nether-plasm.*"

"It looks like it's made out of *bubbles!*" Hannah cried, hugging me.

"The 'bubbles,' Hannah, are fissionable polyps that fuse into whatever physical shape is needed. This is a small Shoggoth, though many different classifications exist. The largest are now the size of office buildings." Kezzy actually rubbed her own boobs while looking at the thing. It just sat there, kind of bubbling.

"It's a *pile of slop!*" I yelled. "How is that thing gonna fuck us?"

"Watch," she whispered, and then the pile started to *shudder*, and *then*....

It started to rise.

I felt stiff as a statue while this pile got bigger before our eyes. I guess *elongate* is the word. It was like one minute there's this bubbling pile of Superballs on the floor and the next minute that pile is...

Standing UP.

In another couple of blinks we were looking at this radiating glop that had sort of taken the shape of a man — er, not really *man* but an upright *thing* that stood on two legs and had two arms and a head.

But it was still made of all those clear Superballs.

"What are all those balls?" I asked. "Are they like...*cells?*"

"In a manner of speaking." But Kezzy couldn't take her eyes

152

Edward Lee

off the smoke, or the image of Curwen's ghost. "The aforementioned polyps. They're fissionable spheroids of ingeniously devised material, ethereally integrated, a non-metallic alloy, so to speak. The most useful morphological configuration is that of a bipedal entity. Wait till the spheroids fuse... And while we're doing that, we have to determine which of you goes first."

"Goes, goes," Hannah stuttered, "g—"

"Which one of us gets *fucked* by it first!" I yelled and, believe me, I knew what was coming. "Go ahead, Miss Kezzy! Let's do it the fair way! Let's *flip a coin!*" Holy *shit*, I was so pissed!

Kezzy's grin was like some evil African mask. The coin glittered. "Call it, Ann."

"Fuckin' *tails!*"

The coin spun in the air, clinked on the floor.

"Awwwwwwww. Heads, Ann." Her eyes beamed at me. "You lose."

"Of *fuckin'* course!"

But in the time it took for me to get shafted again, all those Superballs kind of *melted*, taking on more and more detail, until...

"*There*, ladies," Kezzy celebrated, "is your monster."

I screamed again but Hannah passed out right away. All those Superballs had turned into a monster, all right, and it was standing right there in front of us now. But after the change—the *fusion*—it wasn't clear or slimy anymore. It looked like a man made of raw meat. You ever see a Johnsonville brat before you cook it? Almost blood-red with all these splotches of white fat mixed in? *That's* what the monster—this *Shoggoth*—looked like: a six-foot-tall man made out of Johnsonville brats all mushed together.

But the shape was the only thing man-like. It didn't have fingers; instead, its hands were just these scoop-like things, and the feet were *plops*. The face took longest to form. I didn't see anything like ears, nose, or mouth, but its eyes?

Well, not *eyes*. Eye.

Going Monstering

The eye was the size of a melon. *That* was the face—just that big lidless white eyeball sort of jammed right into the meat where the face should be. There were veins in the eye, but they were all different colors, and the iris was gold.

Then—

I looked between its legs...

"WHAT THE FUCK IS THAT!" I yelled so loud I thought my throat would rip. "Is that its *DICK?*"

The thing sticking out between its legs was made of the same red-and-white meat, only its shape...

It had a shaft, about an inch wide, that was probably ten inches long, but that wasn't the scary part. Instead of a knob on the end there was this big cup, like the rubber cup on the end of a toilet plunger.

"The genitalia of this form of Shoggoth is quite unique," Kezzy explained.

"IT LOOKS LIKE A FUCKIN' TOILET PLUNGER!" I shrieked.

"Actually, Ann, it functions similarly. Upon excitement, the foreskin blossoms into the flexible 'cup' that you see now. You'll understand the complete nature of the process momentarily. But even Shoggoths are sensate enough to seek out a little foreplay, hmmm?"

I just started shivering, paralyzed, when the thing picked me up like I weighed nothing, and laid me down on the slab-like altar. I couldn't look at it, couldn't look at that puckering, one-eyed face, so I closed my eyes and just hoped I would die of a heart attack or something.

Just then Kezzy began reading from the book. I couldn't hear the words but I knew what it must be. *The Ritus Imitor...*

"Watch, Ann. Look at the thurible's smoke."

I turned my head and opened my eyes just for a second. I was looking at that tin ball with holes in it. The smoke was coming out heavier now and it made the image of Joseph Curwen's ghost clearer, almost so clear that he could've been standing here for real. But then Kezzy whispered, "Gleb nub ee-ak, lyrun'b thrubb'k," and—

Curwen's ghost vanished.

But I knew it had gone right into the body of the Shoggoth, and that's when the thing started feeling me up with the scoop-hands...

They were more wet than slimy, like your armpit on a hot day. First they slid up and down my whole body, almost like it was massaging me, then the scoops were playing with my boobs. The sweat coming out of that red-and-white meat must've had something in it 'cos all of a sudden I wasn't scared to death anymore.

I was turned on.

"The discharge from the Shoggoth's sebaceous glands contain arcane libidinal accelerants," Kezzy said, "but this discharge tends to be selective. It indicates that Joseph Curwen *likes* you, Ann. It will make the experience even more ecstatic."

My boobs were tingling like electricity, and then my whole body started to tingle the same way. Then the scoop-hands slid around and started kneading my ass, and eventually one of them began rubbing my pussy.

I started coming in waves. I couldn't even *think* anymore it felt so good. Kezzy said, "The orgasms you're experiencing now are only preludial, but just *wait* till Joseph starts fucking you in earnest with the Shoggoth's cock..."

The thing spread my legs apart and climbed up on top of me. The cup on the end of its cock kind of *sealed* around my pussy, then...

"Get ready, Ann."

When it pushed its cock into me, the cup turned inside-out, and then the shaft went all the way into my cunt. That was all she wrote for my hymen, and it really did *pop*. There was a sound and sensation like when you open a jar of jelly and the freshness seal pops. It hurt like holy hell for, like, one second, and then...

Going Monstering

I started coming again, only it was a hundred times better than before. I could feel the cup—I guess the word is *prolapsing*—prolapsing back and forth with each stroke in and each stroke out. The Shoggoth was doing me real slow and steady, like a machine, and when I finally opened my eyes, I saw its eye staring down at me, all those multicolored veins throbbing. At first I had an orgasm with each stroke, but then it got crazy and I started having one each time my heart beat and, lemme tell you, my heart was beating fast.

It did me like that for, I guess, a half hour, and by then I thought I would just croak right on the slab from all those orgasms.

"Pay attention now, Ann," Kezzy said. She was leaning against one of the pillars, her panties off, playing with herself. "This is the spectacular part."

When the Shoggoth dragged its cock out of me, the cup popped out and was now like it originally was. It fit right back around my pussy, and then I saw the shaft pulsing and then something hot and gushy pushing against my pussy. It was coming now not *inside* me but *outside*, filling the cup up.

That's when Kezzy said, "Shub neb hyr'ik eb hyr'k. Ogthrod ai'f geb'l, ee'h yog-sothoth."

When the Shoggoth pushed its hips forward, the cup turned inside-out again and pumped all that cum right up into me. The stuff felt real thick and was so hot it was just short of scalding. In and out the cup went, just like someone plungering a drain; it even made a *sound* like that...

Only the drain was my womb.

On the last stroke of the cup, I had one great big absolutely insane orgasm, and then that was it for me. I was out cold.

☠ ☠ ☠

Going Monstering

ME and Hannah woke up to the sound of the tires humming on asphalt. We were still naked; Zenas had flopped us both into the back of the Rolls when the final initiation was over.

"Don't mind the mess, girls," Kezzy said up front. Her perfect fucking blond hair was blowing in the breeze from the open window. "Zenas will clean it up like he does every year."

Zenas grunted, but I thought, Mess?

Me and Hannah felt between our legs; then we knew what she meant. The Shoggoth's cum was, like, *stuffed* up our pussies. It wasn't anything like a guy's cum, more like cottage cheese or wet plaster, but it was the color of dark mustard. Some of it was slowly leaking out.

"You'll be busy bees tonight," Kezzy chuckled. "With your douche bags, I mean."

"Fuck, Miss Kezzy. That thing's cum is stuck so far up us, we'll need garden hoses and soup spoons to get it all out, and" — a thought hit me just then, like a lightning bolt. "Holy fuckin' shit! What if we get knocked up?"

"Knocked...up?" Hannah whispered.

She screamed at the possibility, then passed out again.

"Oh, you needn't worry about that. The Shoggoth's sperm is wholly incompatible with human reproductive systems." Kezzy was fussing with her hair. "But there are some useful attributes that the creature's sperm can impart to humans." She turned to look at us. "I'll bet you feel better than you ever have, hmm?"

Actually...I did. Those insane orgasms really tuned me up.

"How long were we passed out, Miss Kezzy?"

"For hours, we're nearly home. Oh, and it's no longer necessary to address me as Miss Kezzy. Just Kezzy from now on, since we're *friends* now."

"So...me and Hannah passed?"

Kezzy frowned. "You'll learn to speak properly soon enough, Ann, but I'm sure what you *meant* to ask was 'Did *Hannah* and *I* pass?' and the answer is yes."

"So, so...we're in?"

"Of course. I never had any doubt at all. And I'm not exaggerating when I say that you are the finest pledge I've ever had the pleasure of knowing. I'm sure you'll make an equally fine Alpha House sister."

I just stared at the moon for a while. *I made it. I'm in...* Then I sat back in the plush leather seat and smiled.

"Why, look at this," she said a few minutes later. "Up ahead, Ann?"

I looked between her and Zenas, and down the road, in the headlights, I could see someone walking on the shoulder.

"There appears to be an underprivileged, lower-economic-status white woman hitchhiking..."

I squinted. "Oh, you mean a white trash bitch, a fuckin' *redneck*."

"Don't you think it would be charitable to give the poor girl a ride? Or might it be even...*better*...to throw Shoggoth sperm on her?"

Fuck yeah! I thought. All I had to do was flex some muscles down there and then a whole handful of the slop squeezed out into my hand. I rolled down the power window and—

SPLAT!

—hit that trailer-park 'ho right in the face. Fuck, the shit hit her so hard she fell down!

Me, Kezzy, and Zenas all cackled laughter.

Epilogue

SO that's my story. That was three years ago, and now I'm about to start my senior year at Dunwich. My grade-point average is 4.0; I'll be graduating a semester early with an honors degree in Advanced Mathematics. I can go to any grad school I want, or just take a job pretty much anywhere with a starting salary of $300,000, but I haven't decided yet. Hannah has a 4.0 as well, Plasma Physics. And you may be interested to know that since that night at the Curwen bungalow, I have never, ever lost a coin toss. If I think tails, it's tails. If I think heads, it's heads.

Every time.

Those subliminal words that Kezzy played on the tape loop, and whispered when the Joseph-Curwen-possessed Shoggoth was ejaculating in me, were this:

"Upon this blessing I *receive* a blessing. I now live to love and serve Yog-Sothoth."

It was a blessing, all right. Hannah and I got the greatest blessing we could ever conceive of. And we found out in short order that Kezzy's spiel about tutorial programs and fitness and nutrition regimens was all a cover story. That Shoggoth's cum was loaded with genetic constituents that effused into our bloodstreams and brains. It gave us photographic memories,

160

off-the-charts I.Q.'s, and comprehension levels like fuckin' Einstein.

Oops. Sorry, I'm not supposed to cuss anymore. It bespeaks coarseness and lack of refinement—not acceptable characteristics of an Alpha House sister. I'm working on it, at any rate.

By the way, two years ago, my parents were both killed in a regrettable car accident. Evidently dear old dad lost control of the Maserati and crashed head-on into a tree. You can pause to wonder about that; I'll simply leave it to your powers of contemplation. I inherited everything but I donated nearly all of the estate to Alpha House. As smart as I am now? I won't need dad's inheritance. Fuck him.

Oops! Sorry...

Oh, and I weigh 118 pounds now. I look a lot like Angelina Jolie but with *much* better breasts. Hannah looks quite a bit like Brooke Shields but when Brooke Shields was, like, fuckin' *twenty*.

Damn! There I go again.

Anyway, the Shoggoth's sperm did more than just make us smart. It *changed* us. It made us *beautiful*. It changed our entire body chemistries. Just more of the blessing of Yog-Sothoth. I read Al Azif every night.

Kezzy visits sometimes from Yale, and we make love for hours on end. When we come, our tentacles just *slide* out of our vaginas and entwine. It feels so *good*.

Oh, here come the new pledges. I forgot to tell you, *I'm* the new Senior Sorority Sister...

"Good morning, pledges. Welcome to Alpha House. My name is Miss Ann—and hear me well when I say *Miss*.... And, *my*, what a ho-hum crew destiny has seen fit to cough my way today, hmm? Why, I'd wager that the four of you together would break a one-ton industrial scale, yes, indeed. Be that as it may, I am your Senior Sorority Sister, and I will be conducting you through this marveling event known as Pledge Week.... But before we begin, would you all like some coffee? Yes? Good! It's preeminent quality—Costa Rican.... There you go, ladies....

Going Monstering

Zenas!"

"Ee-yuh, Miss Ann?"

"Pour the cream."